Sunset Secrets

ANJ Press
Pittsburgh

SUNSET SECRETS
ANJ Press, First edition. March 2022.

Written by Amelia Addler.

Cover design by CrocoDesigns
Maps by MistyBeee

For when what's lost returns

Recap and Introduction to *Sunset Secrets*

Welcome back to Orcas Island! In the last book, Claire Cooke moved to the island after getting a six-million-dollar inheritance. She bought The Grand Madrona Hotel and immediately butted heads with her general manager, Chip Douglas. Then two FBI agents accused her of harboring a dangerous fugitive – a man they claimed was her son.

Claire knew they were mistaken, because she'd never had a son. Twenty-nine years prior, she'd adopted her late sister's three girls – Lucy, Lillian, and Rose – but never a son.

When new information comes to light proving her identical twin sister Rebecca had a son before she died, Claire gets curious. She meets Marty, now the FBI's most wanted criminal, and knows he can't be the dangerous man they say he is.

With Chip's help, Marty proves the CEO from his company, SureFired, framed him as a Chinese spy. The CEO is fired and Marty is hired back to work at SureFired to improve their wildfire prediction technology.

Claire gets her happily ever after when Chip confesses his feelings to her, and they make a pact to run the hotel together.

Marty stays on Orcas Island to get to know his new family, all the while dealing with strange letters and emails from an anonymous source...

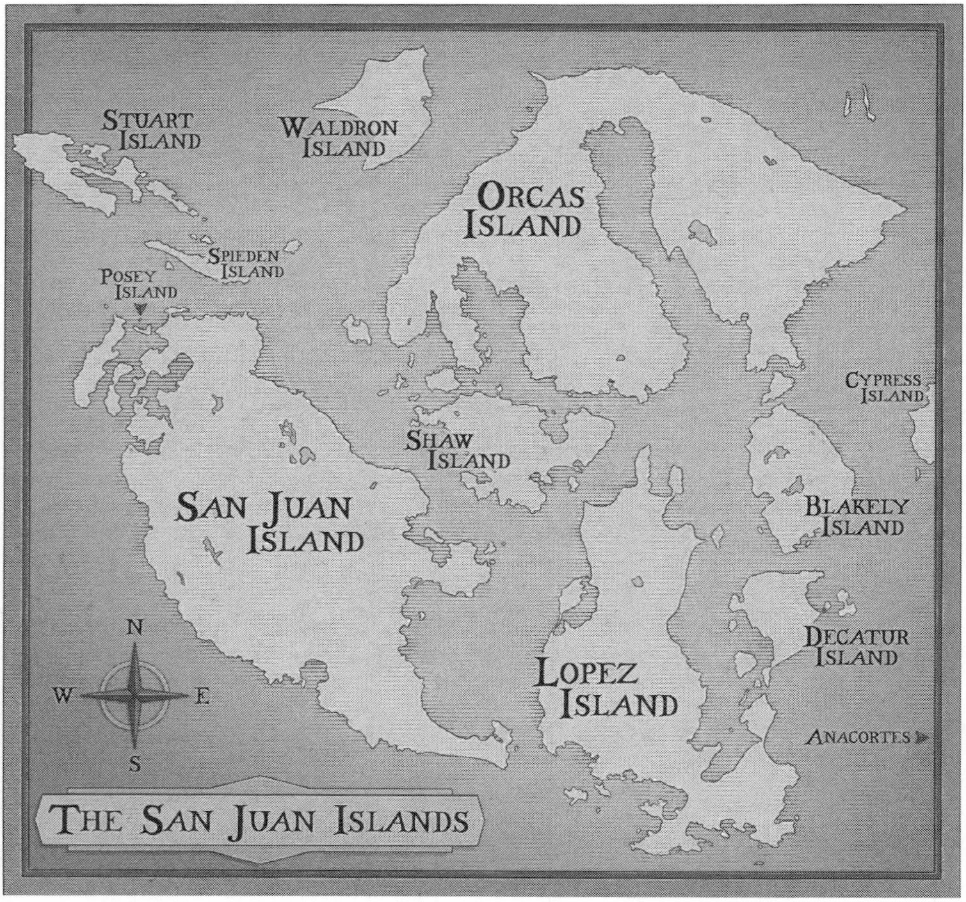
Stuart Island
Waldron Island
Orcas Island
Spieden Island
Posey Island
Shaw Island
San Juan Island
Cypress Island
Blakely Island
Decatur Island
Lopez Island
Anacortes
N
W
E
S
The San Juan Islands

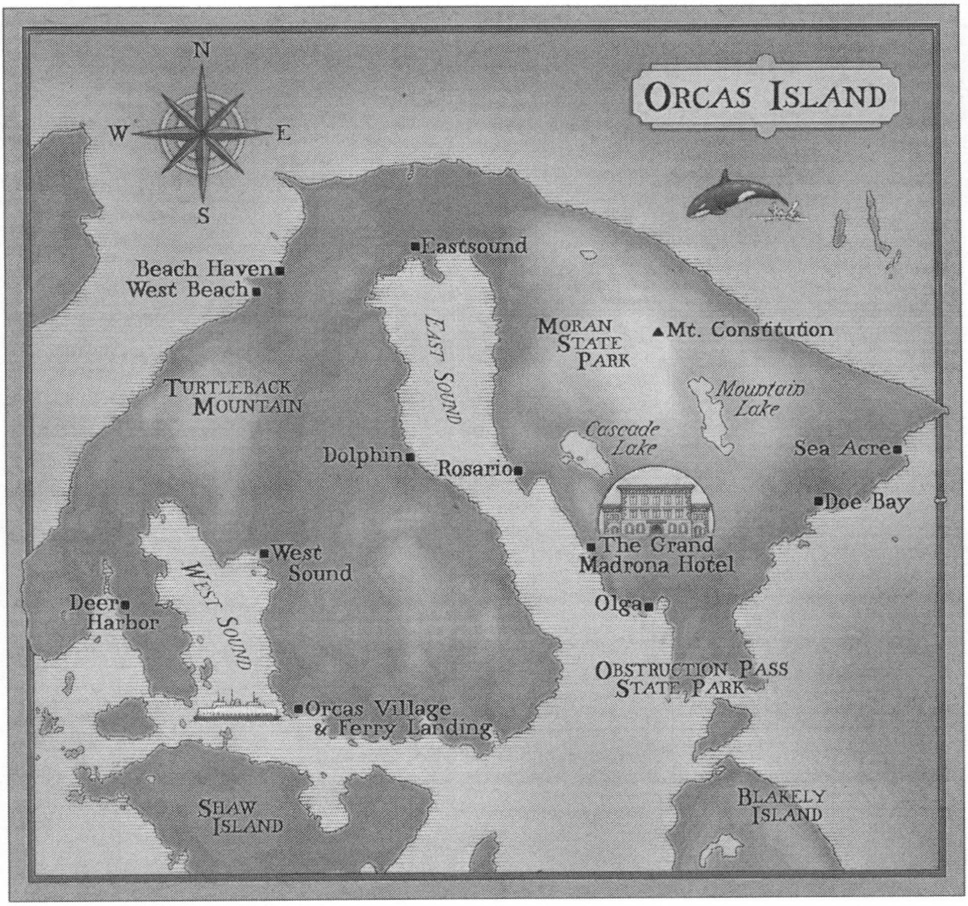
ORCAS ISLAND
N
W
E
S
Eastsound
Beach Haven
West Beach
EAST SOUND
MORAN STATE PARK
Mt. Constitution
TURTLEBACK MOUNTAIN
Mountain Lake
Cascade Lake
Dolphin
Rosario
Sea Acre
Doe Bay
West Sound
The Grand Madrona Hotel
WEST SOUND
Deer Harbor
Olga
OBSTRUCTION PASS STATE PARK
Orcas Village & Ferry Landing
SHAW ISLAND
BLAKELY ISLAND

Chapter One

Mischief-makers and explorers alike often stumble onto the forbidden side of Orcas Island. Taboos are always irresistible, but the forbidden on Orcas isn't a metaphorical place. The bounds are literally marked and labeled.

Marty's first foray into this world was when he traveled to the far side of the island in hopes of exploring a public beach. When he got there, the sun was beginning to set and the beach was packed – all twenty square feet of it.

The public portion was tiny, the width of a single-lane road, and flanked on either side by private beachfront properties. The edges of the public beach were clearly labeled, and for good measure, the homeowners had added their own signs and sharply pointed security cameras. Though the beach went on for miles, there was an invisible line in the sand that made its beauty expressly off limits.

Marty eyed the signs warily, and in an attempt to keep his distance from a pair of beach chairs, accidentally took a step over a property line.

His mistake was short-lived. Moments later, a woman stormed out of the house behind him, yelling wildly and shaking her fist in the air.

At first, he thought she was chasing off a bird. When he realized she was yelling at *him,* he took an exaggerated step over the invisible sand line and smiled, waving back at her. She stared at him for a moment before returning to her mansion.

This woman had spent millions of dollars to live on the water, only to waste her time jealously guarding what was "hers."

How could she own the ocean? The Coast Salish people had shared the islands' beauty and resources for generations. Now they too were forbidden from even setting eyes on entire swaths of forest, stretches of beach, and corners with hidden lakes. The long driveways often hosted a series of increasingly menacing signs.

Private property.

Do NOT enter!

This means **you!**

There had to be a balance of the right to privacy and the pull of the island's rare beauty. Luckily, there were a number of state parks to enjoy, and Marty got another surprise: an invitation to visit an Orcas Island estate owned by the new CEO of SureFired.

Marty didn't hesitate. He treated the reason for the meeting, a discussion of computer servers, like his number-one priority. He cleared his calendar and stressed that he was free anytime, even on the weekends.

When else would he get a chance to walk the grounds of an eleven-million-dollar property?

His Saturday invitation came on Memorial Day weekend, and Marty got to the estate early. He punched in the "secret" code to the gate – 90210 – before driving toward the enormous house looming over the water.

He drove slowly, self-conscious about the rumbling noises his old Kia made. He probably needed a new muffler, but he hadn't cared to fix it until now.

It wasn't that the new CEO, Blaise Krentz, would turn his nose up at Marty's old car. In fact, Blaise drove a beat-up Subaru himself.

Marty respected the Subaru, and even though he was normally wary of any new authority, he had some respect for Blaise in general. The guy had come into SureFired full of ideas and open to feedback. It wasn't lip service; he took employee comments to heart and implemented changes.

Strangely, Blaise had taken a liking to Marty, too. Marty had no idea why, but he didn't question it. It was better than the previous CEO, who had tried to frame Marty as a spy selling company secrets to the Chinese government.

That, and Marty's subsequent evasion of the FBI, had been a low point, though Blaise loved hearing about that time in Marty's life. He said, "Marty, you've got conviction, character, and most importantly, a real backbone – something this industry rarely sees."

Marty wasn't so sure about all that, but he didn't argue when Blaise promoted him to a director position and doubled his salary.

It was, at first, a shock. Marty was suspicious of the promotion. The money was absurd – he had no idea what to do with it. He thought Blaise might be trying to blind him with flattery and keeping him drunk on the almighty dollar.

After working with Blaise for a few months, though, it didn't seem to be the case. Marty still decided to ignore the money, though, letting it pool in his savings and not changing how he lived. He thought it was best to keep things simple.

As long as he wasn't dependent on a high salary, he could afford to speak up again, no matter how unpopular his opinions. He wasn't afraid of getting fired, unless the FBI was sent after him again. It was easy enough to pack up and leave in his old Kia.

He pulled up to the house and realized that there was only one other car there, and it wasn't Blaise's. Marty sent him a message.

"Hey, got here a bit early. I'll be waiting in my car until you get here."

Blaise's response was prompt. "No, please, go on in. The kids are home with Emma, our nanny. I'll let her know you're here."

Marty waited a beat before approaching the magnificent front door. Should he ring the doorbell? He didn't want to wake the kids if they were sleeping.

After some hesitation, he lightly knocked on the rich, dark wood.

A moment later, the door opened, blinding him momentarily. Light poured in from the tall windows that faced the ocean, reflecting beams of sun off of the water into his eyes.

"Hi! You must be Marty."

His eyes adjusted. He expected to see a woman with rosy cheeks and coifed white hair – a grandma, essentially. He'd always been babysat either by his own grandma or a grandma fill-in from the neighborhood.

This woman was no grandma. The light poured in behind her, giving her a sort of glow. Her dark chestnut hair was braided off to the side, and she smiled at him, her warm brown eyes locked onto his face.

Marty smiled back, unable to speak for a moment. Finally, he managed to sputter out, "Hi, Emma, I'm Marty. It's nice to meet you."

She nodded, stepping aside and waving him in. "Blaise said to make yourself at home."

Marty stepped inside, suddenly feeling awkward about his eagerness in coming to Blaise's house. "Thanks."

"I'm just doing some baking with Caleb, and Sophie is taking a nap. Do you like cookies?"

He smiled again. "Yes, I do."

"Great!" She clapped her hands together. "Then we might have something for you guys in a bit. We also might not have anything for you, if things go poorly."

Blaise's five-year-old son Caleb ran over, clutching a measuring cup half filled with flour. He eyed Marty suspiciously.

"Hi," Marty said, kneeling down. "What have you got there?"

Caleb frowned and dropped the measuring cup, dumping flour on the floor as he walked away.

"Caleb, that's not polite," Emma said firmly. "Please come back here and say hello to your dad's friend."

"Oh it's okay – " Marty started, but Emma cut him off.

"He knows better." She crossed her arms and stared at Caleb until he dragged himself back to the front door. "Now what do you say?"

Caleb let out a sigh. "Hi."

Marty felt bad that the poor kid was getting disciplined on his account. "Hi, Caleb."

Caleb looked up at Emma. "Can we bake cookies now?"

She smiled. "Yes, we can, but first, we need to clean up this flour." Emma flashed a smile at Marty before turning and walking back toward the kitchen.

It was an absolute mess, with flour and a pile of eggshells spilling over the kitchen island. Caleb seemed to have his own station where he was mixing something in a bowl. Marty debated how weird it would be if he hung around the kitchen until Blaise arrived.

He decided it was quite weird, especially since he found himself incapable of speaking.

Instead, he saw himself into the living room and took a seat on the couch. Everything in the room was oversized, from the windows to the couches to the luxurious rug.

He couldn't stop staring at the rug. It had to be at least twenty-four feet long. Despite being lush, it did nothing to keep the sounds from echoing against the empty walls.

There were floor-to-ceiling windows that spanned the entire back of the house, offering a brilliant view of the ocean. At this hour, it was not only brilliant, but blinding. There was some sort of a shade, but he couldn't figure out how to work it.

Outside, Marty spotted a large swimming pool, along with what he assumed was a private beach. How many miles of private coastline did Blaise own? The sunsets here had to be amazing.

He was lost in thought when the front door opened and Blaise walked through. Caleb was there in a flash, reaching his flour-white hands up and yelling, "Daddy!"

"Hey Caleb! You're hard at work, aren't you?"

"We're making chocolate chip cookies!"

"My favorite," Blaise said, tousling Caleb's hair. "Hi, Emma. How are you?"

"Good, very good! We're having fun."

Marty stood and walked over, trying not to be too obvious when he stole a glance at Emma. She had a dash of flour on her forehead, but otherwise she looked the same – smiling warmly and dusting her hands on her apron.

Caleb lost interest in the conversation and pulled Emma back toward the kitchen by the hand.

"Marty," Blaise said, "I'm so glad you could make it."

"Thanks for having me," Marty replied. It was strange seeing Blaise out of the office. Though he was a casual sort of boss, it was still odd seeing someone in their home. It was... humanizing. Marty had never gotten to know the old CEO this way.

"Have you had a chance to look around yet?"

Marty shook his head. "Not yet. I was just admiring the view from the living room."

"Let me give you a quick tour then!"

They left Caleb and Emma to their baking as they toured the enormous house. There were six bathrooms, seven bedrooms, a game room, two offices, an elaborate laundry room, and a well-maintained gym. Blaise peered into Sophie's nursery as she slept, and Marty noted that the room alone was almost bigger than his entire apartment.

When they finished, they looped back to Blaise's office. Marty set down his coat and took a seat. "You have a beautiful house. No wonder you encourage everyone to work from home. The office can't live up to this."

Blaise laughed. "It's something, isn't it? Ingrid and I decided to spend the summer here with the kids. We had them signed up at this great daycare, but they had a water main break and had to shut down."

"No kidding."

He shook his head. "It's a bit of a nightmare, but we were able to snag one of the teachers – Emma – as our personal nanny for the next few weeks."

"She seems great," Marty said. He immediately wondered if that was a weird comment to make.

Luckily, Blaise didn't skip a beat. He put a hand over his heart. "She is. She's so great with the kids. Caleb is crazy about her, even though she's pretty strict with him. I could learn a thing or two from her."

Marty laughed. "I'm sure. She's a professional."

Blaise pointed at him. "Exactly. All right, I've got about an hour before I need to meet Ingrid for a pottery class."

"Pottery class?" Marty smiled.

"Gotta keep the spark alive, you know?"

Marty nodded like he knew, though he didn't. In his last relationship, the spark had died before the two-year mark, though they'd held on past their third anniversary.

For a long time, Marty had blamed himself, but now he saw it for what it was: two decent people who simply weren't right for each other.

Blaise and Marty spent the next hour talking about a possible server migration. Marty wasn't against it, but he was clear about the drawbacks. Blaise listened to his concerns and they drew up a document to discuss at the next staff meeting.

Once that was done, Blaise stood from his seat. "I apologize, but I've got to get going. I really appreciate you coming out today."

"It was my pleasure," Marty said, following him to the door.

Blaise pulled the door open to find Caleb's smiling face peering into the room.

"Hi Dad. Can I play golf now?"

"Sure! We're done working." Blaise turned to Marty. "I keep a set of toy clubs in here so he has something to play with when I'm working. So, naturally, it's become his favorite toy."

He laughed as Caleb marched past them, followed by a smiling Emma.

Yes, it was quite something to see Blaise at home. It wasn't the house, so much, that made Marty feel a twinge of jealousy. It was Blaise's family. His kids.

Marty thought that by now he might have had a family of his own. Unfortunately, things hadn't worked out that way. "He's a great kid," Marty said, motioning toward Caleb, who had just made a concentrated swing of his plastic golf club.

"Thank you. We like him," Blaise said with a laugh before giving Caleb a kiss goodbye and thanking Emma.

Marty nodded at Emma before following Blaise out to the driveway. He was in his car, about to pull away, when he realized he'd forgotten his jacket.

Marty changed course, turned off his car, and returned to the large front door. Blaise had already left, so Marty quietly knocked once again.

No answer.

Hm. He waited a minute before knocking a second time. The house was far too large for Emma to hear him, but if he rang the doorbell, he might wake Sophie.

Marty took a chance and tried the doorknob. It was open.

"Hey," he called out. "Sorry! I forgot my jacket."

No response. He made his way back to Blaise's office as quietly as possible.

When he opened the door, he was about to announce himself when he saw Emma planted in Blaise's computer chair, typing away on his computer.

His stomach sank. Marty had been falsely accused of stealing secrets from SureFired, and he couldn't stop his thoughts from going there.

What if Emma wasn't as innocent as she seemed?

Chapter Two

Was it weird to end the email with, "If that's okay?" Emma's mom was always telling her saying stuff like that made her sound weak, but she didn't want to upset Travis. If he got angry at her for the email, then he might not –

"I'm sorry. I forgot my coat," said a voice.

Emma popped up from the chair. "Oh, hey!"

"Hello Marty!" Caleb yelled triumphantly, holding one of his plastic golf clubs in the air and waving it at his guest.

Marty nodded. "Hey Caleb! Looks like you have a good game going."

Caleb nodded and returned to putting.

Emma spotted the jacket draped on a chair and handed it to Marty.

"Thanks." Marty cleared his throat. "I'm sorry, but I have to ask. What're you doing on Blaise's computer?"

Ugh. How embarrassing. "Nothing, really. I just needed to send an email."

He raised an eyebrow. "An email?"

"Yes," she nodded hurriedly. "I just moved to the island to work at the daycare, and I haven't gotten a chance to get internet set up at my place." She paused. That wasn't entirely true.

She couldn't afford internet right now, but Marty didn't need to know that.

"What about your phone?"

"Ah." She pulled it from her pocket, offering it to him. "I make too many typos when I email from my phone." That, at least, was totally true. She was making herself sound insanely guilty for a woman sending an email.

"I see." Marty shifted his weight. "I don't mean to be rude, but do you mind if I take a look? We've had some security issues at SureFired in the past."

Emma was mortified. He thought she was up to no good! Probably because she was acting like she was.

She backed away from the desk, holding her hands up slightly. "No, please, absolutely. Go ahead."

Marty took a seat and ran some sort of command on the computer that she didn't recognize. Was it to see if there any recently closed programs or something?

Emma wasn't sure. She wasn't terribly computer savvy. All she'd done was log on to her email account. Marty could now see the draft she'd been agonizing over.

Her embarrassment was complete.

"Who is this to?" Marty asked with a frown.

She cleared her throat. "My ex-husband, Travis."

Marty's frown deepened. "Who's Dolto? Is that your son?"

Emma wrung her hands together. "No, Dolto is my cat. My husband kept him in the divorce, but I really miss him and, ah, I was hoping he'd let me visit him."

Marty studied her for a moment, his face unreadable. "Your cat?"

She nodded, turning her phone screen on, which had a picture of Dolto as her background. "Yeah. That's him."

Marty stood up and flashed a smile. "I'm sorry. We had some issues last year and I'm always paranoid."

"Oh, I totally understand," Emma said hurriedly. "Blaise told me that one of the employees was chased down by the FBI or something."

"Yeah. That was me, actually," Marty said with a sigh. "It's a long story, but I was innocent."

She put her hands up. "I'm innocent, too. I swear!"

He smiled again. "You are. I'm sorry for interrupting. Have a nice rest of your day."

She smiled and waved, feeling every bit the idiot that she was. Marty had been chased down by the FBI. No wonder he thought she was acting suspicious!

Blaise said she was welcome to use any computers in the house, though. She always logged into the guest account, and it was usually for something simple, like printing things for Caleb to cut out.

This was the first time she'd used one of the computers for personal reasons, and she had been caught instantly. Emma was mortified. She sat in the chair, staring at the screen, trying to regain her composure.

"Did you see that?" Caleb asked, eyes bright.

She nodded. "Good job, bud!"

He beamed, fetching the golf ball.

Emma soothed her nerves with the fact that if Blaise did end up turning her into the FBI, they would see that she hadn't done anything wrong. All they'd see was her slightly pathetic, much belabored email:

"Hi Travis,

I hope you and Kimmy are doing well! I was just sending you a message to check in on Dolto. Did he go to his check-up yet? I know he's due for some vaccines, and I'd be happy to take him. I was wondering if I could stop by and see him sometime? Anytime would work, if that's okay with you!

Thanks,

Emma"

Her last email had gone unnoticed, but maybe Travis had just been busy. It'd been so long since she'd seen Dolto, she was starting to get desperate. Maybe the FBI would take pity on her when they investigated her for this personal computer use on the job.

That made her laugh. If only Travis would take pity on her. That would be enough.

She let out a sigh and hit "send." There went nothing.

Chapter Three

It ended up being obvious that Emma wasn't hiding anything. Marty couldn't help but feel embarrassed for confronting her.

On the other hand, he was entitled to a touch of paranoia now and then. It hadn't been that long since he'd been hunted down by the FBI.

Still. Guilt followed him for the rest of the day. It wasn't just that he had confronted her; he'd also read a rather personal email. He'd invaded her privacy.

What was going on with her ex-husband? Why was he able to hold her cat hostage? The whole thing seemed unusually cruel.

It preyed on his mind all day, and the more he thought about it, the more questions he had. It led him down a rabbit hole.

Marty looked the guy up online and found him easily. There was a lot of public information about Travis Dickinson the Third. He had a Twitter account that displayed his views on football, the weather, and using public toilets. There were pictures of him from his years in a fraternity. On his company's website, there was a warm and fuzzy biography about him and how he found himself in the travel agency industry.

How odd. Marty didn't realize people still used travel agencies.

Travis' online presence didn't stop there. There was also a new wedding registry, complete with pictures of the happy couple. One of the pictures had the two of them kissing, a blurry little brown and white Dolto in the background.

This guy didn't mess around; he was already on his second marriage. Marty hadn't even managed one marriage yet.

Yet Travis was still hanging onto his ex-wife's cat. That wasn't something Marty would do, no matter how bitter the breakup.

In an attempt to forget his interaction with Emma, Marty decided to hike around Mountain Lake. Predictably, the hours alone had the opposite effect. He couldn't stop feeling like a jerk about what he'd done, and as often happened with his negative feelings, he found an exterior place to project them: Travis.

A small scheme hatched in his mind, and once the hike was over, he headed straight home, got on his computer and got to work.

He decided to employ a trick that he'd learned at his old job. Well, not a trick, exactly. It had been part of his responsibilities at that company. He and his team had designed emails meant to test the other employees. Would they click on a shady link or, even worse, would they give up their password?

It was a huge problem for all companies, and the more people they employed, the bigger the problem.

Marty had enjoyed that job. He liked coming up with urgent email subjects that tricked people into clicking.

FWD: HR complaint filed

Password expired – update to maintain access

Puppy found outside, does anyone recognize him?

His emails were so good that he'd gotten people in trouble all the time.

That was what he didn't like about the job. One woman nearly lost access to her email because she got tricked six times. She'd had to repeat Marty's email safety class four times.

"Marty," she once said, shaking her head, "I have your voice in my head telling me not to click on things. But when the subject is so urgent, I get scared and do it again!"

Perhaps now, however, Marty could use his powers for good?

Maybe it was wrong to get into Travis' email, but maybe it wasn't. Something wasn't right about this cat situation. Emma seemed desperate to even see the poor thing.

It made him feel sorry for her, especially after he had insisted on reading her message. He had to make it right.

The email he drafted for Travis was a masterpiece. The subject was "Inappropriate outfits for the office [slideshow included]." He stole the email signature and logo from the travel agency's website.

Inside, he even included a picture of a woman in a too-short skirt. If Travis clicked on it, he'd have the option to view the slideshow as long as he entered his email password.

Marty sent the email off and waited. It could be hours before Travis clicked on it, if at all. He might be waiting for –

Bing.

Marty picked up his phone. He had a hit! It looked like Travis had clicked on the slideshow link three times. Apparently frustrated that he couldn't get past the password screen, he'd finally entered his password on the third attempt.

This was too easy.

Marty quickly got onto his computer and logged into Travis's email account, scrolling through the recent emails. The most recent was the one from Emma. As suspected, it only contained information about Dolto. There were no stolen secrets from Blaise's computer with details about SureFired.

That was good. If Marty were smarter, and less dazed by Emma's smile, he'd argue he'd only hacked into Travis' email account to make sure he hadn't received any company secrets.

That wasn't the case, though. Marty was quite dazed and was acting on something he had no interest in identifying or stopping.

He clicked over to Travis' sent folder. The first thing that caught his eye was that Travis had forwarded Emma's email to someone named flirtybaby994.

He frowned. Who was this? A quick internet search told him it was Travis' fiancée, Kimmy.

His email read, "Should I tell her, or should you? HAHA"

Marty didn't like the tone of that. Tell Emma what? That she was never going to see her cat again?

Marty could feel his blood pressure increasing just as another email caught his eye. This was one Travis had sent to The Grand Madrona Hotel. The subject was "You are at risk of being left off of our recommended list of weekend trips from Seattle."

Talk about pushy. The rest of the email wasn't much better. Travis rambled on about how their company was one of the top results when people searched for weekend trips, and how they helped travelers with the "complicated" ferry system. He said that being left off of the weekend trip list would be detrimental to the hotel, and stated that their agency needed access to special rates for their clients to prevent that from happening.

Nothing like a threat to start a business relationship. Marty went back to Travis' inbox and found that there was a response from Claire.

"Travis,

I certainly don't want to lose business to our hotel! Please tell me what kind of rates you're interested in.

Sincerely,

Claire Cooke

Owner of The Grand Madrona Hotel"

Travis had forwarded Claire's response on to one of his coworkers and added, "Look at this. Another sucker."

Blood pressure officially elevated. It looked like Travis had sent dozens of this same email to hotels not just on the islands, but all throughout Washington, Oregon, and even as far as Montana.

This just wouldn't do. Marty shut his laptop and set off for The Grand Madrona Hotel.

Chapter Four

As expected, Memorial Day weekend brought hundreds of visitors to Orcas Island. Claire was happy with the promotion they'd run for The Grand Madrona Hotel. They were completely sold out of rooms, and the hotel restaurant, The Plum Spoon, had been full every night for a week.

It was her idea to advertise a "kick off the summer" special rate, and it seemed to have worked. Marty had taught Chip how to run specials on websites like Expedia, and off they went.

Claire smiled. She and Chip made a great team. While she was the dreamer, coming up with plans and schemes, Chip was the no-nonsense realist who built the foundation under her ideas. Together, they were unstoppable.

According to Chip, the hotel hadn't seen profits this consistent in over seven years. They were able to hire two and a half more housekeepers, a bellhop, and they were interviewing for a part-time receptionist.

Though the start of her adventure as a hotelier had been rocky, Claire was more grateful every day that she'd stuck with it. She felt like she truly was a caretaker for this beautiful and timeless hotel, and that she'd found her place in the world again.

It kept her busy, too. Their Easter celebration had been a success, and they'd hired a new company to do a light show for the Fourth of July. Claire couldn't wait to see it. It'd be done over the water, and unlike fireworks, wouldn't pose a wildfire threat to the island in one of its drier months.

The Fruit Festival was only a few short weeks away, and though they weren't quite ready yet, Claire was confident that they'd be able to pull it off.

Her personal life was blooming, too. With some convincing, she'd bought a small house in the town of Olga. It had enough rooms so the kids could all visit and stay comfortably, but it wasn't terribly fancy. It made Claire nervous to have both a mortgage on the house and one on the hotel, so she'd tried to keep it simple.

Chip had convinced her it was a good idea, reasoning that she needed to be close to the hotel. He was right. It was convenient to be only a few minutes away from The Grand Madrona, as well as only fifteen minutes from Eastsound for shopping and errands.

He went on to claim that his argument had nothing to do with the fact that he also lived in Olga, and that he could now walk to her house whenever he wanted.

Claire tried to be cautious at first. She couldn't allow herself to be swept up in a whirlwind romance like a giddy schoolgirl.

But it was no use. The whirlwind took them both and she didn't want to stop it. She loved spending time with Chip. He made her world feel whole, and she finally allowed herself to enjoy being in love.

That evening, she and Chip had a reservation at a restaurant in Deer Harbor. After she finished getting ready, she made the short drive to the hotel to pry Chip away from his computer.

When she walked through the front doors of The Grand Madrona, voices and laughter filled her ears. It was a wonderful sound. People were enjoying themselves, talking at the bar and lounging on couches in the lobby. There was even a trio of twenty-somethings posing for pictures with the gorgeous Art Deco staircase as their backdrop.

Claire smiled to herself as she walked through the lobby and made her way to the office. She knocked softly on the door and let herself in.

"Hello, hello," she said as she opened the door.

"Hey, honey," Chip said, looking up from his computer.

"Hey, Claire," Marty said brightly.

She smiled and walked into the room, giving Marty a hug. "I didn't know you were stopping by to see us. Do you want to join us for dinner? We were going to go to the Blue Salmon, but I was thinking I'd rather eat here anyway. We could all eat together."

Marty held up a hand. "No, it's okay. I'm not here to crash your dinner plans."

"He's here to defend your honor," said Chip with a smile.

"My honor?" Claire leaned down to plant a kiss on Chip's cheek.

Marty nodded. "Do you remember getting an email from a travel agency? A guy named Travis Dickinson?"

Claire let out a sigh. "I don't think so. Maybe?"

Chip pulled up the hotel email account. "This one," he said, pointing. "Where the guy threatened to leave us off his weekend getaway list if we didn't comply with his demands."

"Oh right," Claire said, nodding. "I remember that now. He kind of scared me! I looked up the company and they're one of the biggest travel agencies in western Washington."

"Don't fall for it," Marty said. "He sent this same email to everybody. Trust me."

Chip looked over at him. "How do you know that?"

"Don't worry about it," Marty said. "Just don't give in to him. The guy's a jerk."

Claire shot Chip a look and they locked eyes for a moment. "Okay, if you say so. If he writes back, what should I do?"

"Just don't respond," Marty said. "If you want to get on some getaway lists, I can work on that with Lucy."

"Have you talked to her recently? How's Lucy liking her new job?" asked Claire. "I feel like she's not telling me the full story."

He scratched the back of his neck. "Why do you think I would know more than you do?"

Marty was a terrible liar. Something was going on at Lucy's job, and for some reason, she wouldn't tell Claire about it. She'd get to the bottom of it eventually. "Are you sure you don't want to join us for dinner?"

Marty shook his head. "No, it's okay. You two kids have fun."

Chip cocked his head. "Did you just call me a kid?"

"If the shoe fits," Marty said with a shrug.

He waved before ducking out the door.

Claire shut the door behind him and turned to Chip. "He's in a good mood."

"He is." Chip sat back and crossed his arms. "Are you thinking what I'm thinking?"

Claire dropped her voice. "That he has a girlfriend?"

"What?" Chip screwed up his face. "No, not that. He has some sort of feud with this travel agency. Maybe he hacked their computers."

"Oh stop," Claire said. "Marty wouldn't do that."

Chip paused. "Yeah. He probably did it to impress a girl."

Claire took a look at her watch. "All right, log off the computer or I'm going to dinner without you."

He put his hands up and stood from his desk. "Please, Miss Cooke, don't force me to stay here and keep working."

Claire snorted a laugh. "Force you? I can barely pull you away."

He leaned in closer, his face almost touching hers. "You know, there's only one girl that I would hack a computer for."

"Oh yeah?" Claire laughed and gave him a peck on the cheek. "You'd have to learn how first. Let's go, Romeo."

He laughed, grabbing his coat and following her out the door.

Chapter Five

The rest of Marty's week was uneventful. He tried to resist the temptation of clicking into Travis's email again, but it was too hard. He had to see if Travis had responded to Emma.

When he popped into the email, he saw there was no response. Apparently Travis had read her polite plea and completely ignored it. What kind of monster was this guy?

Marty was happy, at least, that he could keep Claire from being duped by him. If only there were something he could do to help Emma.

He kept hoping that he'd catch sight of her in town, or at the grocery store, or anywhere, but she was nowhere to be found. Blaise probably kept her busy with the kids all week.

On Friday, Marty finally had a stroke of luck when Blaise mentioned his computer keyboard had stopped working. While he could buy something on the island, he admitted that he preferred an Apple keyboard.

"I have an extra. I'd be happy to bring it over," Marty said. It wasn't an extra, exactly. It was the one that he used most of the time. He'd be happy to get a cheaper one for himself, though, if it meant a chance to see Emma again.

Blaise offered to stop by and pick it up, but Marty insisted on dropping it off. He claimed he'd be in the area and Blaise accepted.

Marty set off right away so he wouldn't lose his nerve. He realized this might be the last chance he had to see Emma naturally, and he was desperate to find a way to see her again. It was hard for him to sleep. He was constantly thinking about her, and her little brown-and-white cat.

He made up his mind that he was going to ask her out, somehow. Marty wasn't particularly suave, but if he set his mind to it, he thought he could do it.

He arrived at the estate far too quickly, and as he drove toward the house, he realized he felt far less dazzled than he had the first time. These estates weren't all they were cracked up to be. The grandeur had to get boring, didn't it?

He walked up to the front door, keyboard tucked under his arm, and knocked. After a moment, the door opened. He looked down to see Caleb beaming with pride.

"Hello!" Caleb called out merrily.

"Hi again," Marty said. "May I come in?"

Caleb turned around, apparently seeking approval from someone behind him. Finally he said, "No," and shut the door.

Marty laughed. A moment later, Emma opened the door, shaking her head. "I'm sorry about that. He's a bit frenzied right now."

Marty waved a hand. "That's fine. I just stopped by to give this to Blaise." *And to have an excuse to see you again.*

"Right, he mentioned you were coming. I can give it to him."

Marty hesitated before handing it over. "Also, I wanted to apologize for the last time I was here. You know, with the computer and your email...."

"Oh!" she smiled. "It's totally fine. I get it. No harm done."

"No. It was rude, and I'm sorry." Marty cleared his throat. "I've been thinking a lot about that email."

A crash rang out behind them and Emma turned to see Caleb giggling and running away from the vacuum cleaner. "Do you want to come in for a second?" she asked.

"Sure."

He stepped inside, watching as Emma wrangled with Caleb's wild mood. It took her a few minutes to get him settled into a less destructive activity – coloring. Sophie was sitting in a high chair, happily picking at scattered cereal.

"Sorry about that," she said when she returned.

"No problem. I'm the one interrupting here."

She crossed her arms. "You said you were still worried about my email?"

He shook his head. "No, not worried about the email, per se. I think I'm just more curious, I guess."

She eyed him. "Curious?"

"Not to be nosy, but I've been playing the scenario out in my head all week." He paused. Was he taking this too far? It was too late now, and he had nothing else to go off of. "I've been imagining this dramatic divorce hearing, your cat between you and your ex-husband in a cage, being pulled back and forth until the judge hits his gavel, and then we hear a meow."

Emma laughed. "That's not quite how it went down."

She'd laughed! That was good. It bolstered his confidence. "The thing is, now I can't stop coming up with my own story for how it happened."

She rubbed her face with her hand. "It's not really a story. We got divorced, he got the cat, and... that's it."

Shot down. Marty couldn't let it go. "Really? It was that simple?"

She laughed again and let out a sigh. "You're right. It wasn't that simple. It's just an unpleasant sort of story."

"Ah. I see." He paused. He'd pushed it too far. It wasn't charming to force someone to talk about their painful divorce. "I can tell you about my most unpleasant story – the time I was living in the woods hiding from the FBI."

She narrowed her eyes. "Were you really hiding in the woods?"

"Yeah. I can show you where I camped. I hid in the state park. I hike there now. Fun memories and all."

Emma uncrossed her arms, studying him. "I can't tell if you're being serious."

Marty had that effect on people. "I am one hundred percent serious." He put his hands up. "I swear."

She picked up a crayon that had rolled away from Caleb. "It sounds like you had fun."

He laughed. "Maybe, looking back, I did. I mean, I must've liked the island enough. I ended up moving here."

She nodded.

"It's a great place." He was babbling, but he couldn't stop. "Have you gotten a chance to go to Moran State Park?"

She pursed her lips, thinking. "Is that where you camped?"

He nodded. "One of the places, yeah."

"No, not yet. I haven't really seen anything."

"Does Blaise ever give you time off?" Marty asked. "Should I talk to him?"

She smiled, shaking her head. "No, don't do that. I get time off. I have tomorrow off, actually. It'd be nice to explore the island a little."

Was that a yes? Or even a maybe? "I could show you around the park, if you'd like. We could go for a hike."

Emma stared at him for a moment before responding. "Sure. Why not?"

"Great. How's ten?"

"That works for me." She paused. "Is it easy to find?"

"Yeah, there's only one road in the park. We can meet by Cascade Lake. There's a nice hike there."

She nodded. "That sounds good. I'll see you then."

Marty was amazed he was able to pull that off. True, he'd started off poorly, demanding she tell him about her divorce – that wasn't great – before talking about his life on the run.

It was one of the only things she knew about him, though, and likely the most interesting thing about him. It had worked, at least. Perhaps he wasn't the most charming guy, but he'd managed to ask her out in the end.

He decided to leave before he accidentally made things worse. He handed over the keyboard and made a quick exit.

Part of him wished he'd gotten her phone number in case she decided to back out. On the other hand, Emma didn't seem like the sort of girl to stand a guy up. Marty smiled to himself and started his car.

Chapter Six

It wasn't a bad idea to make a friend on the island, was it? Marty seemed nice enough, and though Emma didn't know how long she'd be living on Orcas, putting down roots would make things easier.

She'd applied to the job at the daycare on a whim. The salary was much higher than any of the daycares near her home, and it looked like they employed a wonderful early education model.

Plus, she'd felt suffocated at home. If she wasn't running into Travis, she was running into reminders of her old life with him. It was impossible not to; they'd been together for nearly eight years.

It was sort of a wild idea to move all the way to Orcas, and it was unlike her to be wild. Yet she had gone to the interview, had loved the staff and the island, and... here she was.

Her afternoon with the kids went smoothly. Caleb got over his brief chaotic spell, and Sophie continued being her cheerful, sweet self.

Ingrid got home early and relieved Emma of her duties.

"Now you can get an early start on the weekend!" she said.

"Thank you. I really appreciate it," Emma replied.

She meant it. She didn't know Ingrid and Blaise well, but so far, they were one of her favorite couples to work with. The kids were wonderful, and Emma had plenty of freedom in deciding the activities to fill their days.

Even when Ingrid and Blaise worked from home, they made a point to avoid hovering or micromanaging. They trusted her to take care of the kids, and were polite and respectful of her time. To top it all off, they paid her almost double what she had been paid as a nanny back home.

That night, she went back to her apartment, made some mac and cheese for dinner, and settled in front of the TV. She liked having the noise in the background as she looked up information about the island.

Emma found the park that Marty talked about – Moran State Park. There were two lakes, Cascade Lake and Mountain Lake. She'd forgotten which one she was supposed to meet him by. Was it Cascade? That was the one near the entrance of the park, so she would start there.

She lost interest in her show as she read more about the peaks and hikes. Turtleback Mountain, which was on the west side of the island, supposedly had the best views. The tallest point on all of the San Juan Islands, however, was Mount Constitution.

The mountain was in Moran State Park, towering above the lakes at an elevation of nearly twenty-four hundred feet. In the 1930s, the Civilian Conservation Corps had built a watchtower at the summit. It offered a full three-hundred-and-sixty-degree view of the islands. Emma made up her mind that she wanted to go to the top, even though heights made her queasy.

She read on, learning about the man who originally owned the land, Seattle shipbuilder Robert Moran. He'd retired to Orcas in 1906 when his health declined, believing he only had six months to live.

Either the fear was unfounded or the island saved him, because Moran survived for nearly four more decades. When he met the so-called Father of National Parks, John Muir, Moran decided to sell much of his estate for public use. His land, sold to the state of Washington at a bargain, became a state park in 1921.

Emma was fascinated with Moran's history. He'd arrived in Seattle at the age of eighteen with a few pennies in his pockets. He'd worked tirelessly, creating a successful shipbuilding business, and eventually was elected mayor. He was in charge when the Great Fire hit, and spearheaded efforts to modernize Seattle's water supplies.

Emma felt a kinship to Moran. They'd both fled the hustle and bustle of Seattle, and though Emma had arrived nearly broke on Orcas, she tried not to let it get her down. As Moran once said, "Money represented no value to me excepting as a means to carry on an industrious life."

She liked that. Emma drifted off to sleep, smiling to herself, her mind filled with thoughts of what it would've been like to live on the island in 1906.

She got to the park early the next morning. Almost as soon as she passed under the white arch at the entrance of the park, she came upon Cascade Lake and pulled into a parking spot. There was an option to pay for a single day or for a season-long pass. Hopefully she'd be on the island long enough to enjoy the season. She opted for the pass.

Despite the early hour and chill in the air, there was a lot of activity at the lake. People were pouring out of their cars, some dressed in hiking gear and being dragged by their dogs onto trails. Others were wrestling kayaks off the top of their cars or herding groups of children in swimsuits toward the small, roped off beach.

The lake was surrounded by hills covered in trees, giving it a cozy, tucked-in look. Emma was surprised by how tall the trees were. She'd read that many had been cleared out for logging, so they couldn't have been terribly old.

They were gorgeous, though, and she alternated between admiring them and standing at the water's edge, looking down through the perfectly clear water.

Marty arrived after not too long and found her standing at the dock.

"I'm glad you made it!" he said.

She turned around and smiled. "Me, too. This lake is unbelievable. It's so clear!"

He nodded. "It is."

"You camped here?" she asked, tilting her head. "It looks pretty busy."

He laughed. "No, I stayed deeper in the woods. Though this is especially busy, being a holiday weekend."

"Ah, right."

"Do you still want to hike here? We could find a less popular trail."

She shook her head. "No, this is perfect. I could just stare at the lake all day."

"That's an option too." He paused. "There's a great view from a wooden foot bridge not too far from here, if you're up for it?"

It was getting chilly just standing around. Walking would keep her warm, and she didn't mind a hike. "I'd love to see it."

They strode past the playground and onto a trail that hugged the lake. Spring was breathing life back into the island, and Emma savored the earthy scent of the forest.

"So, I have to ask," Marty said, once they had been walking for a few minutes. "Is Travis going to let you see Dolto?"

Emma stared down at her feet and her steady steps in the dirt. "I haven't heard back from him yet, but I'm hoping I do soon."

She clenched her jaw, trying to force the tears to go back to wherever they'd come from.

It was hard. She missed Dolto endlessly. She'd raised him from a baby. He had been only a few weeks old when she'd found him, and she'd stayed up day and night, bottle feeding him.

She'd lived in the dorm then, and had to hide him until she could move into an apartment. At the time, she and Travis were dating, and he said she was a fool to move to a more expensive place for a cat.

Emma didn't see it that way, though. It was just money, and Dolto was her best friend. When she woke up in the morning, he'd be there, quietly staring at her. After she opened her eyes, he'd let out a little chirp or bop her gently on the head. They would snuggle every night, with him laying on her lap or her chest or anywhere else he could fit. She missed his sweet face and the way his purrs centered her on even the worst days.

Emma cleared her throat. No need to get choked up now. It was hard to explain to someone who probably thought she was just being crazy about a cat.

"I'm sorry," Marty said softly. "I always had cats growing up. I know what it's like."

She looked over at him. "Really?"

He nodded. "Oh yeah. My mom's a huge animal lover. She'd come home with a new cat every couple of years. She'd find them on the road, or someone at work would hear meowing in a pipe and bam! New cat. At one point, we had six at once."

Emma laughed. "That's a lot of cats. I've only ever had Dolto."

"It seems especially mean that Travis won't let you see him."

Emma shrugged. "He's not a mean person, not really. But..."

They stopped at an outcropping to catch their breath where a gorgeous tree had grown over the lake.

Marty leaned against it. "But what?"

She shrugged. "Travis always had a mean streak. Sometimes he can be petty. He never really turned it against me, though. Not until, you know. We got divorced."

"I'm not trying to pry," Marty said. "It just seems odd that he won't even let you visit."

"I think it's partially because of his new fiancée. Even though we're broken up, she feels threatened by me in some ways. She has no reason to get jealous. I'm not trying to win him back, but it's been an issue. He doesn't want me to upset her."

Marty smiled. "She could just give you your cat back and then you'd have no reason to talk to him."

"Yeah," Emma said, shaking her head. *If only*. "I can understand why she feels that way. Travis and I were college sweethearts. We met freshman year, fell in love, and got married right after we graduated. I'd just started my master's degree when..."

She stopped herself. Marty was easy to talk to, but he didn't need to know her whole history. If he knew the truth, he would only feel sorry for her. Emma hated it when people felt sorry for her.

"When things sort of fell apart?" Marty offered.

"Yeah." That was one way to put it. Everything fell apart then. She had been diagnosed with a bile duct disease called primary sclerosing cholangitis. She'd never heard of it before, and could barely pronounce it. She'd gotten so sick that she'd had to drop out of her program.

It wasn't until she was approved for a liver transplant that Travis broke the news he couldn't stay with her. It was too much for him – all of it. It was a long, terrible journey that neither of them had planned to take.

"I'm sorry. I don't mean to dredge up old memories," Marty said. "I know how hard it is to lose a pet."

"Thanks. Yeah, it's hard. It's actually nice to be able to talk about him," she said with a smile.

No one else in her life wanted to hear her talk about Dolto. Her dad told her she was fixated on her cat instead of worrying about saving her marriage. That wasn't true, though.

Travis had made it clear that he couldn't stay with her. He said that when they got married, it was with the understanding that they could start a family. Her going through a transplant had ruined that future for him.

Though the doctors said she could likely still get pregnant, it was more dangerous. She was at higher risk for infections and complications; she also had to be on anti-rejection medications for the rest of her life.

As much as it hurt, it was impossible to argue against. There was a chance she'd never be able to have kids, and that was too much for Travis to get past. So she let him go.

Marty spoke again. "If there's anything I could do, please tell me. Really."

"I wish there was. Thanks for the offer."

He seemed like a nice guy. Not that she was in the market for nice guys. It was embarrassing enough that her marriage had failed. She wasn't going to repeat that mistake again. Some people just weren't meant for love.

Emma walked away from the grand tree and back toward the trail. "Now tell me about this FBI business."

He laughed. "All right, as long as you're ready for a crazy story."

"I've been dying to hear it," she said, hopping from rock to rock. She meant it. Marty seemed like he could be a friend, and Emma felt lucky to have the chance to get to know him.

Chapter Seven

The trail grew steeper and Marty did his best to talk without sounding too breathless. He told Emma everything, from the Thanksgiving where his drunk aunt revealed he was adopted, to putting his DNA in that online registry, to getting locked out of the SureFired office.

"Wait, you left the building one day and then you couldn't get back in?" asked Emma.

"Yep. That's exactly what happened," he said.

He went on, telling her how he'd rushed home, forgetting his wallet, and went into hiding. He told her about finding a match for his mother in the DNA system, looking Claire up, and traveling to Orcas Island on a whim.

He pulled out his phone to show her the various spots on the map where he'd camped for a few weeks until meeting Claire and finding out that she wasn't, in fact, his mother.

"So the DNA company was wrong?" Emma asked.

Marty shook his head. "Not exactly. This is where the story gets even more wild."

He told her about Claire's identical twin sister, the plane crash, and how everyone in her family had passed away that day except for the three nieces she'd adopted.

By this point, they'd reached the beautiful wooden bridge. Marty leaned against the railing and looked at Emma; she leaned forward, hands over the side, staring into the crystal-clear water.

"I know this sounds entirely made up," Marty said. "But I swear it's all true. I have proof."

Emma laughed. "I believe you. Though it does sound like a movie."

"They say the truth is stranger than fiction."

Marty was glad to see Emma smiling again. He could tell that talking about Dolto was difficult for her. He hadn't meant to push the subject earlier, and was happy to tell her anything she wanted to know, even if it was a wild or embarrassing story from his past.

Emma turned and leaned back against the wooden railing. "Now I feel like I have to tell you more about my life. It's not really fair."

He waved a hand. "It's not a competition."

Marty was actually a tad embarrassed. He was so desperate for Emma to find him interesting that he'd basically told her his entire life story.

He usually didn't talk to people about his run-in with the FBI. It was too outlandish, and too personal. True, Blaise loved it and would ask him about it at the office, but even most of his coworkers didn't know the full truth.

What had gotten into him?

He crossed his arms. "I'm hoping the rest of my life is uneventful."

She laughed. "So your tombstone can say, 'He lived an uneventful life, except for that one time'?"

"Yes."

Emma looked him in the eye, then down at her shoes. "I can tell you more about my life, but only if you promise not to feel bad for me."

"Feel bad for you?" He frowned. He already felt bad that she had a schmuck of an ex-husband who'd stolen her cat.

Emma nodded. "Just promise you won't, okay?"

Marty caught her gaze again. He'd do anything she told him to do. "I promise."

"It's not nearly as bad as what happened to you," she said, "but the reason I didn't fight for Dolto in the divorce was because I was dealing with a lot."

"I'm sure," he said.

She continued. "I was in my first year of my master's program in teaching. Things were going well, but then I started to feel sick. I was really itchy and I'd have night sweats, so I went to the doctor and tried everything – creams, changing my detergent, all kinds of allergy pills."

Marty tilted his head to the side. "That's weird."

Emma nodded. "Travis thought I was just stressed from school, but my mom really wanted me to get it checked out, so I kept going back. The doctor said it was probably nothing to worry about, but eventually, I found out that I had primary sclerosing cholangitis."

"What's that?"

"It's a disease where your bile ducts get inflamed and scarred, and eventually it leads to liver failure."

"Liver failure?" His eyes were wide. He didn't mean to sound surprised. She looked so healthy.

"Yeah." She let out a sigh. "You said you wouldn't feel bad for me."

He put his hands up. "I don't! It's just surprising. I've never heard of that before."

"It's so rare, most people have never heard of it. They didn't suspect it in me, either, because I have no other illnesses and there was no sign of *why* it happened. It just did." She clenched her hands together. "I had to drop out of my program because I started to get weak."

"Of course! How could you stay in school?"

"Right? Honestly, though, as far as illnesses go, it wasn't that bad. I got sick so quickly that I was moved up the transplant list, and I was matched with a donor. My recovery wasn't bad, and now I'm as good as new."

Marty felt like the wind had been knocked out of him, but it was just Emma standing there, smiling at him. "That's a much wilder story than mine."

"No, not really." Her smile slowly faded. "It was during that time that my marriage started to fall apart. Things were so hectic. I know it's dumb now, but I didn't get my own attorney and...well, somehow the paperwork said that Travis got to keep Dolto."

Marty's jaw tightened, but he said nothing.

Emma brushed the hair out of her eyes. "It was just a bad time. There are things I regret, but I can't go back. I think that Kimmy, Travis' new fiancée, really likes Dolto. He's such a great cat. I mean, who wouldn't fall in love with him? He's so sweet, and funny, and smart..."

This guy divorced his wife when she needed a *transplant?* He couldn't believe someone could do that and go on living with themselves.

Marty tried to tactfully keep the emotion out of his voice. "Can you get a lawyer now? To get Dolto back?"

She shook her head and laughed. "I don't have money for an attorney, and I'm not sure there's anything they can do."

"Oh."

"I'm not destitute or anything," she added. "It's just that I'm still paying off bills from the hospital, and there was that time I had to be hospitalized after the transplant, so yeah. It adds up."

Medical debt. What a nightmare. "I'm sorry. That just stinks."

"Tell me about it."

"Do you have school loans, too? Maybe you could consolidate and refinance."

She bit her lip. "Well, I don't have school loans, but in the divorce, I got half of Travis' graduate school loans, so there's that."

Marty realized his breathing was getting heavier. If he ever ran into this dude...

She put her hands on her hips. "I feel like I'm talking negatively about Travis, and I don't mean to. I don't want to be a bitter ex-wife."

Marty smiled. "Believe me, you don't come across as bitter at all. It seems like you're too nice, honestly."

"That's what my mom always says," Emma said with a laugh.

Don't offer to pay for a lawyer. Don't offer to pay for a lawyer. "I'd be happy to hire a lawyer. Not for you. For Dolto, and for all of cat kind."

Emma let out a loud laugh, scrunching her nose. "Ha! That's very sweet of you, but I couldn't accept that."

Marty figured she wouldn't take it, but he had to offer. What was his new salary good for if he couldn't put it to use?

"It's so beautiful here," she said. "The view is just breathtaking. Does the trail go on?"

Marty nodded. "It goes all the way around the lake and gets pretty steep. Do you want to do the whole loop?"

Emma smiled. "If you have time...?"

For her? "I'm free all day."

"Let's do it then!"

The hike took almost three hours. They stopped to admire the view several times, and Marty got to play hero when he pulled snacks from his hiking pack.

When they got back to the parking lot, they said their good-byes and Marty made sure to get Emma's phone number.

On his drive home, he replayed everything Emma had told him about her divorce. He managed to keep his promise. He didn't feel sorry for her. He felt angry for her, which was a much more useful emotion.

Once home, Marty went straight to his computer. He got into Travis's email and started digging. Searches for "Dolto" and "cat" didn't reveal much. The emails were mostly from Emma.

Next, he started reading through Travis' sent emails. As it turned out, he didn't reserve derogatory remarks for The Grand Madrona Hotel.

Oh no. Travis made fun of coworkers, customers, and even his boss. He had a flagrant disregard for his own career, sending these emails from his work account. Marty would never dream of saying half of these things, let alone on company property.

If working in tech had taught him anything, it was that nothing was secure on a computer, especially in a company-owned email account.

Most recently, Travis had forwarded an email to a coworker calling the CEO of the travel agency a "sniveling, clueless fat cat" who was "impossible to underestimate." He continued that "everyone who ever loved him was wrong," and that the day he died would be a blessing to the company.

Marty knew he shouldn't do it. He knew it was wrong, and that two wrongs didn't make a right but...

With a few clicks of a mouse, Travis' bold email was forwarded to everyone else in the company.

Computers could be so glitchy like that.

That was the end, though. Marty logged out and promised himself that he wouldn't log into the email again.

Chapter Eight

The daycare was supposed to open again on Monday, but Emma's boss told her things had taken an unexpected turn for the worse. It looked like they'd be closed for another week.

Emma didn't mind it much. She loved spending her days with Caleb and Sophie, and after her hike with Marty, she was inspired to show them the sites of the island.

With Blaise's blessing, she decided to take the kids to Cascade Lake on Monday. Blaise thought it was a great idea; he even gave her a stipend for outings going forward. He told her to use it to cover snacks and activities, as well as her cost for gas.

Emma was surprised and delighted by this. Gas was extremely expensive on the island, and the extra money meant they could do more exploring.

They got to the park early, and Emma was pleased to see it was far less busy than before. There were enough kids on the playground to keep Sophie interested. She was happy to spend some time on the swings or lounging in her stroller, watching the kids or looking up at the trees.

Caleb enjoyed the playground as well, running around like mad, until Emma called him over to try his hand at fishing. They didn't catch anything, but he liked holding the worms.

On their way home, Emma got a call from Travis. She didn't answer it – she was driving – but she got a bit excited. It had been months since he'd called her. Perhaps he'd changed his mind about letting her see Dolto?

When they got back to the house, Sophie went down for her nap and Caleb requested to play with his trucks. Once Emma had everything settled, she gave Travis a call back.

He answered right away, his voice heavy. "Hello?"

"Hey, Travis. Sorry I missed your call. How are you?"

"Not that great. I lost my freaking job."

Emma gasped. "I'm so sorry. What happened?"

"My boss is an idiot, that's what happened."

She heard a loud crash, followed by the sound of Travis cursing.

"Are you okay?" asked Emma.

"Not really, no. I just smashed my knee." He sighed. "Your cat's at the vet. He's been having diarrhea all over the place."

Her heart sank. "What's wrong with him?"

"They think he swallowed a toy or something. They want two thousand dollars before they'll even consider operating on him to pull it out."

"Two thousand dollars?"

"Yeah, Emma," he said. "Pets cost money, and now that I lost my job, I can't afford to keep taking care of him for you."

"I'll take him back," she said quickly. "I'm happy to."

Her mind was going a mile a minute, and her hands suddenly felt hot. What could Dolto possibly have swallowed?

He'd never done anything like that before; he didn't even try to steal treats when they were in reach. He was such a good cat.

"You can't take him from Kimmy. He loves Kimmy."

Emma fumbled with her purse. "Where is he? I can go there and pay."

"There's no time for that. Do you have the money or not? Check your account and let me know if you want to do the surgery. The other option is euthanasia."

Emma sat down. A wave of heat and nausea washed over her.

There was no need for her to check her bank account. She always knew exactly how much money was in there, especially after her move to the island.

Her checking account had $128. On Friday, she'd get paid for two weeks of nannying – a hundred hours – and that'd be another $1,749.

Rent was due at the end of the month, though, as was her health and car insurance, and her loan payments. After all of that, she'd have $257 left over.

Moving had been expensive, and she'd hoped to add more to her savings with her salary from the daycare. With it being closed, though, that hadn't worked out yet.

Her savings account had $2,160.

She cleared her throat. "I have the money. I'll pay for it. When do you need it?"

"Like yesterday," he said. "They won't do anything unless they have the full payment up front."

Emma looked over at Caleb, who was still playing with his trucks, blissfully unaware of her crisis. "I'll send it right now."

"Okay, thanks."

He ended the call, and Emma used her shaking hands to navigate to her banking app. She moved two thousand dollars from her savings to her checking account, and then sent it to Travis with one click.

Emma didn't care about the money. Well, she did – her savings was her emergency fund and her ticket to reapply to school, but she cared far more about Dolto than she did about any of that. She could always make more money; she could never replace Dolto.

Emma fetched a snack for Caleb and then sent Travis a text. "Did you get it?"

He replied a moment later. "Yeah, thanks."

"Let me know when he goes into surgery, and as soon as he comes out, please?"

No response. Emma didn't want to be too distracted, so she set her phone aside for an hour as she and Caleb colored. Then, after Sophie woke up, they all played nicely on the living room floor. Sophie had a small, musical keyboard and Caleb had Play Doh.

Things were so peaceful that Emma took the opportunity to call a few emergency vets in Travis' area. On her third call, she struck gold.

The receptionist, Carly, was quite kind despite sounding stressed. She confirmed that Dolto was there and that he was doing better.

"We still haven't gotten payment for the surgery," she said. "That is, if he still needs it. The doctor will be around again in a few hours to reassess him."

"Travis should be coming in to pay soon," Emma said. He was probably waiting until after traffic died down. If only Emma had called and made the payment over the phone....

"Okay, perfect," Carly said. "I'll let the doctor know. Dolto is doing really well, by the way."

Emma's chest tightened. "Really?"

"Oh yes!" She laughed. "He's been curled up in my lap for the last hour, batting at my ID. He's the sweetest little guy."

"Yeah, he is," Emma said. "Thank you for taking such great care of him."

"It's my pleasure."

They ended the call and Emma felt like she might cry. At least it sounded like Dolto was in good hands. Maybe he really would be okay?

It wasn't until that evening that she got a response from Travis. It was a text with a picture of Dolto, and though his belly was shaved, he otherwise looked well.

Travis' text read, "He's home, and he's fine."

"Thank goodness!" Emma wrote back. "Can I stop by and see him this weekend?"

"We're busy this weekend," he said. "Maybe some other time. Also, please don't text me. Kimmy doesn't like it."

Right. She was supposed to stick to email. She could do that. At least Dolto was okay. And Travis was talking to her again. She could work with that.

Now all she had to do was figure out her finances.

That evening, she scoured the help wanted ads and online postings for part-time jobs nearby. There were a few jobs on San Juan Island, but the commute would eat up too much of her time. She applied to a handful of positions and went to bed, dreaming of Dolto purring on her lap.

Emma was surprised when she got a call for an interview the next day. It was for a hotel on the island looking for a part-time receptionist on the weekend.

"That would be perfect!" Emma said, agreeing to meet them for an interview in two days' time. It had to be in the evening because of her nanny duties, but Blaise said it was no problem and said she could even leave a bit early.

She didn't tell him that she was interviewing for another job. It was still her hope that they'd keep her in mind for nannying once the daycare reopened.

On Thursday afternoon, Emma drove straight from nannying to the Grand Madrona Hotel. She pulled into a parking spot and tried to touch up her hair; Caleb had accidentally dunked a strand in maple syrup and it still looked a bit wonky.

She fixed it as best as she could and then, since she was early, she decided to look around outside. The hotel was a grand place indeed. There were two tall Madrona trees in front of the elegant building. Their red, outer bark was peeling off in sheets, exposing the white bark beneath. Emma paused on her way in to feel the coolness of the white bark. Rumor was that the bark stayed cool even on the hottest of summer days.

When she got inside, she went to the front desk as instructed and let the receptionist know that she was there for an interview.

"An interview?" The woman crossed her arms. "I hope you're not coming to steal my job."

Emma smiled. "No, definitely not. The posting was for part-time work. To fill in, I think?"

A smile spread across the receptionist's face and she stuck her hand out. "That's right. I'm Gigi. Nice to meet you."

"It's nice to meet you, too. I'm Emma."

Gigi crossed her arms again. "So just weekends and stuff, right?"

Emma nodded. "I think so."

"Good." Gigi snapped her gum. "I'm sick of working weekends. I'll let the bosses know you're here. Do you mind manning the desk for a minute?"

This seemed like a test. "Of course not."

Gigi smiled and walked off.

Emma wasn't sure if going behind the desk would be crossing the line, so instead, she stood off to the side, trying to look friendly and helpful. Luckily, though people were walking through the lobby, no one stopped at the front desk in need of assistance.

Gigi returned a few minutes later with two people. One was a tall, middle-aged guy with dark salt-and-pepper hair and dark eyes. Gigi was talking to him, but he didn't seem to be paying her much attention. He was more focused on the woman to his left. She was closer to his age, with delicate features and bright green eyes. Emma could see her warm smile from across the room.

"You must be Emma!" the woman said. "Thanks so much for coming in. I'm Claire, the owner of the hotel, and this is Chip, my manager."

Emma shook both of their hands. "It's so great to meet you. This hotel is so beautiful."

"Thank you!" Claire said. "How about we give you a tour, and then we can sit down and talk?"

"Sure!"

Emma was always nervous for interviews, but talking to Claire and Chip made her jitters melt away. As they showed her around, they asked her what brought her to the island and about previous jobs she'd held. Emma admitted she had no experience in hotels, but she had a lot of experience in customer service.

They walked her through the halls and showed her a guest room, then the banquet hall and the restaurant. They told her about perks like free meals and flexible scheduling.

At the end of the tour, Emma found herself outside on the patio overlooking a gorgeous view of the water. It was quite stunning; she lost her train of thought for a moment, just in time for Claire to ask her if she had any questions. Emma was embarrassed that she did not, and she said as much.

Claire laughed and waved a hand. "That's all right. I know how stressful interviews can be. I used to dread going to them."

She smiled. "Well, I'm ready to start the interview now, I think."

"You already answered everything I wanted to know," said Claire. "The question is: do you think you'd like working here?"

Emma almost gasped. Chip and Claire had been so casual that Emma didn't even realize she was being interviewed. "Yes! I would love to! I can start as soon as you need. I'm free this weekend, and I'm free in the evenings, too."

"Talk about a go-getter," Chip said with a laugh. "Addie, one of our other receptionists, is scheduled this weekend. She's very thorough, so I'd prefer for her to start your training. That is, if you decide to take the job."

Emma couldn't believe they were offering her the job! "That sounds perfect."

"Well, great!" Claire said. "How about you think about it, and I can get a written offer to you tomorrow? You can give us your answer when you're ready."

"Oh, right," Chip added. "Don't feel like you have to decide by this weekend."

Emma didn't have to think. This place seemed lovely. "That works for me. Thank you both so much!"

Emma left the hotel feeling better than she had in weeks. The pay was decent, and it would help her get back on track with her savings. It'd be a bit tiring to work every weekend, but Chip and Claire seemed like wonderful people and the hotel was so neat.

Emma's life on the island was headed in the right direction.

Chapter Nine

"I really liked her," Claire said when they got back to the office.

Chip nodded. "Me too. I'm glad Gigi didn't scare her off."

"Gigi's not *that* bad," Claire said with a laugh.

"No, she really is," Chip said. "But it's nice of you to pretend otherwise."

Claire crossed her arms. "Can you tell me why you're sitting at your desk when we were supposed to be leaving for Marty's?"

"I just wanted to check a few things..."

Claire shook her head. "No. No more things today. You're turning into a workaholic!"

"It's hard not to when things are going so well," he protested, but he stood up from his desk. "I'm afraid of dropping the ball and ruining everything."

"You can't ruin anything. The hotel probably doesn't even need us much anymore," Claire said with a smile. "Let's go."

They made the drive to Marty's apartment and ended up being three minutes late. Claire apologized as soon as they got inside.

"It's totally fine," Marty said. "I fell a little behind on the risotto anyway."

"Oh, risotto!" Chip sat down, admiring the spread. "You didn't have to get fancy for us, Marty."

Marty laughed. "It's not that fancy. It's from a box, though it does require a lot of stirring."

The main course was a baked chicken parmesan – a new recipe Marty had wanted to try out. He'd called Claire to tell her about it, reasoning that it was too much to make just for himself.

Claire didn't need an excuse to hang out with Marty. She'd accepted his invitation without hesitation. He could've been serving them bowls of cereal and she still would've been happy to stop by.

"How are things at work?" she asked.

"Really good, actually. I've been working with Blaise on upgrading our systems. It seems like things are moving in the right direction."

"Is this guy on the up-and-up?" asked Chip.

"It seems that way." Marty paused. "Though to be honest, I never fully trust anyone anymore."

Claire frowned. "That's sad. You have to give people the benefit of the doubt sometimes."

Marty stared at her for a beat, then smiled. "Do I?"

They laughed. The food was delicious and Marty liked the bottle of local cider that Claire had brought along to share. It didn't really pair with the food, but she wasn't sure how that even worked. She made a mental note to talk to the manager of The Plum Spoon to get some pointers.

After they cleared the table, Claire excused herself to use the restroom. On her way back, she caught a glimpse of a new framed painting at the edge of Marty's bedroom. "What's this picture, Marty?"

"Oh, it's something a friend sent me. Hang on, I'll tell you about it in a second."

She stepped into his bedroom and turned the light on. It looked like an old-timey picture of Seattle, except there was a Godzilla scaling the Space Needle. It was quite cute.

Claire was continually surprised by how neat Marty was. There was only one area in his room that looked messy: a pile of papers on his TV stand. They looked like they were about to slip onto the floor.

Claire walked over to straighten out the pile. Most of the papers looked like boring mail – coupons and bank statements – but one caught her eye. It was third from the top, a short letter that read:

Dear Marty,

I caught you on the FBI's most wanted list last month. You look so much like someone I used to know. I'm here for you if you need me. Take care and stay out of trouble.

Yours,

B

She was rereading it when Marty walked in the room. Claire jumped in surprise.

"Sorry. This stack looked like it was about to topple over."

"I need to get to those." He waved a hand. "Isn't this painting cool, though?"

She left the papers and joined him in front of the picture. "Oh yes. Very cool."

"My friend sent it to me. I think it's hilarious. He got it from a company in Pittsburgh. They do these sort of alternative history pictures. Do you think the hotel needs one?"

Claire laughed. "As much as I like them, I don't think so."

"Too bad," he said.

"Where's that dessert?" Chip called out from the other room.

Marty started back towards the kitchen, calling, "Who said anything about dessert?"

It was a bluff. She knew he had brownies and ice cream for them. Claire took a deep breath and followed him to the kitchen. She wasn't sure what was more mortifying, the fact that Chip was in there demanding ice cream like an overgrown child, or that Marty had caught her snooping around his room.

She hadn't meant to snoop! It was just her urge to tidy things up that drew her deeper into his room. She shouldn't have even stepped foot in there.

"How many scoops of vanilla do you want, Claire?" Marty asked.

"None, thank you. I'm stuffed."

She didn't want to overstay her welcome, so as soon as Chip finished his dessert, they left. On the drive home, Claire told Chip about the letter.

"Doesn't that seem odd?" she asked.

Chip shrugged. "Who knows what it was about? Maybe it's a letter from an old girlfriend."

"I don't know," she said with a sigh. "It gave me a weird feeling. I know Marty mentioned that he got fan letters after being one of the FBI's Most Wanted, but this just seems off. Why would he keep it?"

Chip shrugged. "Who knows? It's probably best to forget about it."

Claire knew he was right, but it didn't mean she'd be able to follow his advice.

It felt too silly to even say out loud, but the letter B made her think of her twin sister Becca. Claire *knew* Becca had died in that plane crash. She knew she'd been gone for nearly three decades.

And yet...

Claire pulled out her phone and sent a text to her friend Margie asking if she'd like to get lunch soon. If anyone would be up for a scheme, it was Margie.

Chapter Ten

The weather was magnificent that week, and Marty used it as an excuse to go hiking every day after work. It was a fitting explanation, though it didn't totally cover his ulterior motive —taking pictures to send to Emma. His hope was that he could entice her to go hiking with him again if he showed her enough beautiful places.

It was lame, and Marty knew it, but he wasn't the most accomplished flirt. His last relationship had started when his girlfriend had asked him out. He'd liked her, but he'd been too shy to make a move.

Emma didn't seem like the type to ask a guy out, so Marty had to adapt. He went to Turtleback Mountain one day and got a picture from the top of Ship's Peak. The view was unparalleled, with islands and sparkling water as far as the eye could see. The climb was admittedly a challenge, but Emma said it looked like it was well worth the effort.

That was enough encouragement for Marty. He then went to one of his favorite spots on the island: Obstruction Pass State Park. There were a few trails throughout the park, as well as campgrounds that overlooked the stunning rocky coast below.

Marty carefully took pictures of the deserted beach, walking up and down multiple times, the smooth stones shifting under his feet. He had to be careful getting around a few piles of bone white driftwood; at one point, he'd stood atop a large log and almost toppled down when the pile shifted.

No harm, no foul. The sky was a shining, clear blue, making the scene only more pristine. He spent half an hour getting the perfect pictures, even catching a few sea otters frolicking by the rocks.

It was worth the trouble. Emma loved the otters, and she said the beach looked like something too perfect for this world.

Marty saw an opportunity, but he didn't want to be too forward. He struggled with what to text her, eventually settling on, "We should hike here together sometime."

Her response came quickly. "I'd love that!"

Where to go from there, Marty wasn't sure, but he was happy they were talking. He also asked her about the kids, what activities they were doing, and how repairs were going at the daycare.

He steered clear of bringing up Dolto, figuring that if she had any good news to share, she'd tell him. There was no need for him to poke at the wound.

Also, true to his word, Marty didn't go back into Travis' email. He felt a bit bad about what he'd done.

Well, not *that* bad. Travis had said all of those things. It wasn't like Marty had made them up.

Yet still. Marty knew it was wrong. Sometimes his temper got the best of him. It was a flaw and he knew he needed to work on it.

Hiking helped. It made him more present, and it built up his courage. On Thursday, he decided to give Emma a call.

Horrifyingly, she picked up. "Hey Marty!"

"Emma! Hey!"

"What's going on?"

Marty cleared his throat. "Not too much. How're you doing? How're the kids?"

"Oh, really good. They loved going to Cascade Lake this week. I was planning on asking you if you knew any other child-friendly spots."

A request! "Yeah, I do. I could make a list for you."

"That would be so helpful!"

He didn't know why, but it was much harder for him to ask her out this time than the last. He killed time chatting about some spots on the island, but finally forced himself to say what he'd been meaning to say. "You know, the weather this weekend will be perfect for hiking. Would you want to do something?"

Emma groaned. "I'm sorry. I wish I could, but I'm starting a new part-time job this weekend. Just for some extra cash, you know?"

"Oh yeah, totally, I get it. No problem. Maybe some other time."

"Yes. We'll have to find a good time."

He ended the conversation soon after so he could spend the next hour replaying it in his mind.

Maybe she was just too nice to tell him to buzz off? That made sense, and he decided to leave her alone for a while. If she even wanted to be friends with him, she'd reach out again. If not, then he'd take the hint.

Claire needed him that weekend anyway. She wanted to add a section to the website for special events, and while she hadn't wanted to ask him to do it, after Chip had told him about it, Marty volunteered.

He was happy to help. It was easy enough, and he didn't want some stranger messing up the work he'd put into the hotel's website.

On Saturday, Marty planned to do one of the shorter hikes on Mount Constitution, but first he stopped by the Grand Madrona to get details on the update.

He walked in the lobby, suddenly noticing the mud caked onto his hiking boots, and was shocked to see a new face behind the reception desk.

He thought he was hallucinating at first, but no, it was her. Emma, clear as day, eyes locked on the computer screen in front of her.

Marty couldn't stop himself. He quietly walked up to the desk and rang the bell.

Both Emma and Addie jumped at the sound.

He laughed. "I'm sorry. I didn't mean to sneak up on you."

"Hey Marty," Addie said, flashing a smile.

Emma's mouth popped open, then formed into a broad smile. "Marty! What're you doing here?

He crossed his arms. "I should ask you the same question." He tried to look annoyed, but it was too hard. He was elated to see her. It also helped his confidence that she smiled when she saw him.

"I work here," Emma said.

Marty leaned on the counter. "So do I."

Addie giggled. "He's the owner's nephew."

Emma put her hands on her hips. "What? You never told me that."

Marty shrugged. "You didn't tell me your new job was here, either. I thought I told you that Claire owned the hotel?"

"Oh, I guess you did." Emma frowned. "I just didn't make the connection that it was *this* hotel."

He was about to speak again when Claire appeared. "Hey Marty! Thanks for stopping by. This is Emma, our new receptionist."

"We've met," Marty said with a nod. "We have the same boss, technically."

Claire looked at him, puzzled.

"We do, I guess," Emma said with a laugh. "I've been nannying for Blaise Krentz after the daycare sustained some water damage."

"Oh!" Claire nodded. "I heard about that. What a nightmare."

"It's been a mess," Emma said. "But Blaise and his wife Ingrid are wonderful. And Marty introduced me to Cascade Lake. The kids loved it!"

Claire smiled. "That's one of my favorites. Is that where you're headed today, Marty?"

"No. Today I'm going to Mount Constitution."

Claire clasped her hands together. "Oh, Emma, you'll have to see that too. Marty would be happy to show you around, I'm sure."

Embarrassment flooded into Marty's cheeks. He didn't think Claire meant to do it, but it happened nevertheless.

He cleared his throat. "Did you want to talk about those updates in your office?"

Claire nodded. "Ha. My office. I still think of it as Chip's office."

Marty started walking off, hoping Claire would follow. "Have a nice day, ladies."

Claire walked behind him and kept chatting. "You don't have to do this today, obviously, but you can use my computer if you'd like."

Marty would love an excuse to stick around the hotel longer. "Sure. That sounds good. I'll try to get it done today."

"I had no idea you knew Emma," Claire continued. "Why didn't you tell me?"

"I didn't know you hired anyone." Marty paused. "And... you know."

"Know what?" Claire turned to face him as they reached the office door. "Oh no." She dropped her voice. "Do you not like her? When we interviewed her, she seemed so sweet."

Marty shook his head. "Nothing like that. I like her a lot. You just...yeah, you definitely should've hired her."

A small smile settled on Claire's lips. "I see."

Here we go again. Marty didn't know how to deal with this, so he opened the door and said hello to Chip.

"Hey, it's the computer guy," Chip called out. "Are you here to save the day?"

Marty laughed. "I guess so."

Claire pulled up a second chair to her desk and they both took a seat. She said nothing else about Emma and instead focused on the list of events she wanted to add to the website.

"We have some old pictures for them, but I don't know if they're worth using. or if it'll even make sense to add them."

He nodded. "I'll see how it looks."

"You don't have to do this today, or at all," Claire continued. "I know it's a lot of work."

"It's really no problem," Marty said.

"Are you sure? It looks like you're ready to hike a mountain. I don't want you to waste your weekend."

"It's fine," he said. "It'll take me like half an hour. Really."

She smiled. "I really appreciate it, Marty. We'll pay you for your work."

"Please don't insult me with that," Marty said with a laugh.

"Yeah, Claire, don't insult the man," Chip added. "His work is priceless."

Marty chuckled. "Exactly."

Claire had to meet with an events coordinator and left them both in peace.

Chip and Marty chatted for a bit but then both turned to work quietly at their respective desks.

The update wasn't much trouble at all. Marty spent most of the time figuring out how he wanted the layout to look. He settled on one that highlighted a number of pictures. They were decent in quality and made the hotel look lively.

He was almost done making the page when his phone dinged with an email. Normally he'd ignore it and try to focus on the task at hand, but one of the graphics was being annoying and he wanted to take a break.

He picked up his phone and saw that the email had come into his work account.

That was odd. Blaise didn't like people working on weekends.

Marty opened it and realized that it was from an unknown address. The subject was, "Related?"

His hands went cold as he read on.

Hi Marty,

I heard your history from a friend. I know about the FBI and all of that, but I was most interested in the story about your mom and that plane crash. I think we might be brothers. Or at least half-brothers. I know how crazy this sounds, so I don't expect you to answer. I just wanted to say hello.

It wasn't signed. The email address gave no hint to the person's name.

Marty opened a new window on the computer and tried to track the email, but it was untraceable. If this guy really was his brother, he was pretty clever.

Dang.

This was crazy. His first instinct was to tell Claire, but he stopped himself. He didn't want to upset her until he knew more.

He thought about answering right away, but decided it might be prudent to sit on the email before coming up with a response. As shown by the Travis incident, Marty sometimes acted too brashly. If this guy really was his brother, he didn't want to mess it up.

At that moment, Claire walked through the door. She had uncanny timing.

"How are things going?" she asked.

Marty clicked back to the hotel's website. "Good. I'm almost done. Do you want to see it?"

"Sure!"

He clicked around, showing her how visitors to the site could navigate the links and events.

"This is amazing, Marty! I'm always so impressed with you."

"Thanks," he said. "I'm almost done, so I think I'll finish it up at home later." It was too hard for him to focus on this now.

"No problem. You know, I thought of a way to repay you."

He smiled. "Free lunch at The Plum Spoon?"

She shook her head. "No, something better. Chip, did you know that Marty and Emma are friends? Maybe we could let her out of work early to enjoy a hike with Marty!"

Oh dear.

Chip shot her a look. "That's a terrible idea. She needs to learn the booking system while Addie's here to teach her."

Claire waved a hand. "It's not that hard. Even I was able to learn it from Gigi."

Marty was already backing his way out of the room. Though Claire's heart was in the right place, he didn't want Emma to feel like her employment at the hotel was contingent upon her spending time with him. "Chip's right. It'd be better if it were some other time. Enjoy the day!"

He got out of the office before Claire got any more ideas, shutting the door firmly behind him.

On his way out, he hesitated. On the one hand, he could sneak out of the back and not have to see Emma again.

On the other hand, he wanted to see Emma again...

Marty straightened himself out and headed toward the lobby.

Chapter Eleven

Chip was right. Addie was a great teacher, and she made Emma feel like it wouldn't be long before she'd be able to run the front desk on her own. The hardest thing would be fielding off-the-wall questions from guests, but Addie assured her that Chip and Claire were always available for help if something came up.

Emma was admittedly a bit distracted after seeing Marty. It was surprising to see him and find out that he was Claire's nephew. That was all.

When he had walked away, Addie let out a big sigh. "Isn't he so cute?"

"I guess," Emma said with a shrug.

Of course Emma thought he was cute, but it seemed wrong to admit it. What if Claire heard? Wouldn't she think less of her? Also, if Addie had a crush on Marty, it meant he was off-limits.

Not only that. He was off-limits because Emma was a divorcée who had exactly none of her life put together. She was struggling to get by and had perhaps foolishly moved to an island far from all of her family, friends, and support.

Her illness had made her more bold than she used to be. There was an urge to live fully, and that might've been why she surprised even herself by her most recent move.

Yet, even still, she couldn't possibly handle a relationship, no matter how cute or nice the guy was. Addie could date Marty. She *should* date him! Emma wouldn't get in the way. She didn't have time to swoon over Marty. If she had enough time to swoon, then she had enough time to find a third job.

Despite Emma telling herself all of these things, she couldn't help looking up from the desk every few minutes, checking if he was around. It wasn't until she was taking a phone call that he stopped by the reception desk again.

Emma smiled at him, then reassured the woman on the phone that she wouldn't have to worry about tsunamis if she came to visit.

The woman began a story about how she'd almost drowned as a little girl on a Florida beach once. Emma wanted nothing more than to politely cut her off and say goodbye, but she knew it wouldn't work. People could always tell when she was trying to get them off the phone, and their indignation at the fact only made them ramble more.

She mouthed "sorry" at Marty. He smiled, his sharp green eyes twinkling at her as he kept talking to Addie, his voice low.

Finally, the woman finished her story and was reassured enough by Emma's insistence that she said she'd think about booking a room.

"Sorry about that," Emma said once she hung up the phone.

Marty shook his head. "I don't know that she's going to believe you."

"I don't know either," Emma said.

"You forgot to tell her that you're a tsunami expert, and that you've been studying at the Tsunami Institute for ten years," he added.

Both Emma and Addie laughed.

Addie, ever full of insight, offered her take. "Sometimes, if you get a rambler like that, you can interrupt them and say that you have to put them on hold for a moment, that you're going to check something for them."

"Check what?" asked Emma.

Addie shrugged. "It doesn't matter. After they're on hold for a few minutes, it'll make them lose their train of thought. Then all of a sudden they're annoyed that you're wasting *their* time, and they don't keep telling you whatever story they were going on about."

"That's brilliant," Emma said.

Marty nodded. "Nice one, Addie."

Emma's eyes darted between them. She told herself not to feel jealous. Why shouldn't Addie date Marty? They seemed to like each other, and so what if Addie worked for his aunt? Marty didn't seem to care. Claire clearly liked Addie.

"What're you doing here today, Marty?" asked Addie, leaning forward on the desk.

"Not much. Claire wanted some help with the website. I'm trying to maintain it for her."

Emma cleared her throat. "So you're kind of like a consultant for the hotel?"

He laughed. "I wouldn't say that, but I think Claire needs more help than she's willing to ask for."

"I could see that," Addie said. "I could give you a list of things that guests have complained about on the website."

Marty raised an eyebrow. "Really? That would be helpful, honestly. I could come in once a week and address those things."

Addie smiled, dropping down to pull a notebook from her bag. She opened it on the desk and added "List of complaints for Marty" on her to-do list.

Marty looked at Emma like he was going to say something, but all he said was, "Thanks, Addie."

She smiled. "No problem."

"I'll see you guys later," he said, turning to leave. Then he paused and spun around. "Actually, Emma, I'm hiking Mount Constitution today. I can send you some pictures from the top if you'd like?"

Emma couldn't help it. She broke into a wide smile. "I'd love that."

Once he had disappeared through the front doors of the hotel, Addie crossed her arms and stared at Emma. "You like him, don't you?"

"No. We're just friends," Emma said, busying herself with straightening out the pens and papers scattered about.

Addie laughed. "Honestly, good luck. I've been trying to flirt with him for weeks, but it never seems to work."

Emma found that hard to believe. "Really?"

Addie let out a sigh. "Yeah. It's okay. I think he's just nice to everybody."

"He does seem really nice," Emma said quietly. "He's been helping me with adapting to living on the island."

A smile spread across Addie's face. "Let me know if that *adapts* into anything more."

Emma rolled her eyes. "Oh, stop."

As promised, after a few hours, Marty sent along pictures from his hike on the mountain. He admitted he didn't hike all the way to the summit – he'd driven there – but said it was only because he didn't want to get caught out after dark.

"Also, I'm super lazy," he admitted.

Emma laughed as she typed out her response. "You're not lazy at all! You've been running around all day."

"I only drove here so you'd have the benefit of seeing what you're missing," he wrote.

Emma smiled to herself. That was nice of him. "I can't wait until I get to see it myself!"

She worked at the hotel on Saturday and Sunday, and on Monday she was back at the daycare. It was a bit hectic adjusting to the new schedule, but the week went well, and on the weekend she returned to The Grand Madrona for more training. This time she was working with Gigi, who was a lot less friendly than Addie and more inclined to leave her unattended.

Emma didn't mind that too much. She felt comfortable doing bookings and using the computer, and Marty stopped by again with plans to tackle a list that Addie had left for him.

He offered to take her to the restaurant in the hotel on her lunch break. The prices looked far too rich for Emma, but as if reading her mind, Marty reminded her that she got one free meal per shift.

"I'm not saying that because I'm too cheap to pay for your meal," he said with a laugh. "I'd be happy to pay, but you're entitled to your benefits."

Emma smiled. "I can't say no to that."

When they walked in, it was obvious that Marty knew all the servers and everyone they saw greeted him warmly. He was quite the popular guy, it seemed.

They were seated quickly and Emma was overwhelmed by the choices. She settled on a lunch special that included an albacore poke salad, duck fat french fries, and smoked black cod.

Every bit was exquisitely done. She would've been happy with just the salad, or just the fries, but everything together? Phenomenal. Emma couldn't remember the last time she'd had such a fantastic meal, and in unladylike fashion, she ate everything on her plate.

Between bites, she asked, "Does Claire own the restaurant too?"

Marty shook his head. "No, she just rents the space out to the owner of The Plum Spoon."

"Does that mean she has to pay for my meal herself?" Emma set her fork down.

"She gets a huge discount," Marty said, waving a hand. "She's happy to do it. I know I'm biased because we're related, but she's genuinely a great person. Just don't ever tell her I said that."

Emma smiled. Though she was mortified that Claire had to pay for her meal, Marty's jokes seemed to make things just a tad better. "Don't worry. I won't say a word."

For the next four weeks, they continued this pattern, with Emma working every weekend and Marty coming in to do projects. They had lunch every time, and Emma got to know the menu at the restaurant quite well. It came in handy when guests had questions about the restaurant, and Emma never missed a chance to talk about how lovely the food was.

It was nice spending time with Marty, but Addie's words rang through her head: Marty was just a nice guy and she shouldn't read too much into their hangouts.

Emma knew it was for the best, even if she had a tiny crush on him. She wasn't ready for a relationship now, or perhaps ever. Her divorce had been the single most painful thing that had ever happened to her.

A liver transplant was one thing. It was terrifying, it was physically exhausting, and she had literally feared for her life.

The divorce was... something else. It not only destroyed her future, but it also felt like it ripped apart the impression of her past. It made her feel like a fool, like her entire world had been built on sand that washed away at the first crash.

She tried not to think too much about it. She was slowly building her savings back up, and she was having fun with Marty. Even on days when she was exhausted from working so much, she was happy to see him. He made her feel like moving to the island wasn't a mistake, and that was enough for now.

Chapter Twelve

It was getting harder for Marty to pretend he had things to do at the hotel. He'd completed everything on Addie's list and even added a "Historic Orcas Island" section to the website, much to Claire's delight.

Though he could continue to tweak things, he was desperate to come up with new excuses to see Emma. She was working so much that she always declined his invitations for dinner or to go hiking.

Marty finally saw an opportunity when Emma mentioned she needed to make a trip to the mainland.

"How much are ferry tickets for a round-trip car ride?" she asked on Sunday.

"Fifty-four dollars," he said.

She winced. "Wow."

"I have a pass for the season, though," he lied.

In truth, he'd thought about getting a pass, but rarely left the island, so it was a waste. He'd happily get one now, however.

He spoke again. "I've got to use up five round trips before September."

"Oh, really?" She poked at her lunch sandwich. "I wouldn't want to take up one of your trips."

"Please, I haven't used a single one yet. I'd be happy to take you. I've been meaning to go into the office to pick something up anyway." That was sort of true. He wanted to see if he could find out any more about that weird email he'd gotten from his "brother." He had access to more tracking tools in the Seattle office.

"When were you planning on going?" she asked.

He shrugged. "It's not urgent, so I was waiting for a convenient day. Do you need to go soon?"

Emma nodded. "Yeah. Travis called, and he needs the key to our old storage unit."

"Can't you just mail it?"

"Normally I would, but he said that he absolutely needs it on Monday and I have to meet them there."

Typical Travis, making demands. "Why is it so urgent?"

She took a sip of soda. "I'm not sure. He lost his job recently, and we have some old furniture in there that he wants to sell, so that's probably it. I don't want to fight with him about it. It's not worth it."

"Lost his job, huh? What happened?" Marty tried to pick up his coffee in a casual way.

"I'm not sure. I think he got into a fight with his boss."

Marty started coughing, almost choking on his coffee.

"Are you okay?" Emma asked.

He nodded, holding a hand up and forcing himself to drink water to clear his throat.

Perhaps he had gone too far with Travis' email. Not because Travis didn't deserve it – his boss now knew what a jerk he was. Marty hadn't invented any of that. The problem was the unintended consequences on Emma.

"Why don't you tell him you'll bring the key if he brings Dolto?" Marty asked.

Emma looked down, her long lashes closed for a moment. "Wouldn't that be great? Travis isn't one to respond to threats, though."

Marty had to hold his tongue. There were a lot of things about Travis he didn't like, but Emma wasn't one to speak poorly of others. She insisted on taking the high road. Marty could probably learn a thing or two from her. "Well, Monday's great for me."

Her face brightened. "Really? You don't mind?"

"Not at all. Honestly, I was dreading driving out there by myself. It'll be fun. We can make it a road trip."

"I'll pay for gas," she offered.

Marty shook his head. "Please, don't worry about it. I had to make this trip anyway."

Plus he knew that Emma was cautious with money. Why else would she have gotten a second job at the hotel? She worked all the time. It made Marty feel guilty about his recent raise.

He'd already tried to campaign for Emma to get a bump in her pay at the hotel. Claire wasn't opposed, but Chip thought she should at least be out of training before she got a raise.

Such a stickler, that Chip.

"What time do you want to leave? I can check the ferry schedule."

"I took the early shift at the daycare, so I'm free starting at three."

Marty nodded. "Perfect."

As soon as he left the hotel, Marty went to the car wash and frantically vacuumed and cleaned his car. He wasn't a slob or anything, but with all of the hiking he'd been doing, the floor mats had far too much mud and dirt on them for his liking.

Once that was done, he was quite pleased with his old car. He checked the oil and the tire pressure and topped off the gas. He debated getting an air freshener, but thought that might make things worse. Instead, he treated the seats with an upholstery spray, which made the entire car smell more pleasant.

The ferry departure was tight with their schedule, so Marty picked Emma up from work and they went straight to the ferry terminal.

He'd packed a small cooler in the back with drinks and snacks, though he wasn't opposed to stopping along the way to get dinner.

Once they were on the ferry, he suggested they get dinner out if they had time. He had a place in mind that was delicious, fast, and a touch romantic.

Emma hesitated. "Only if you let me pay for it."

He shook his head. "Sorry, can't. My invitation, my treat."

"I guess we're not going, then," Emma said, crossing her arms.

He should've seen that coming. Marty got nowhere in arguing with her and eventually agreed to her terms. He mentally switched restaurants to a place that was less expensive. It was still nice, just not as romantic.

Emma was happy once he agreed to it; she said it helped her feel better about mooching off of him for the trip. If only she understood how much Marty was looking forward to it...

They hit some traffic on the way down, but luckily the storage unit was north of Seattle, so they weren't stuck for long.

They arrived about twenty minutes early. Marty was curious to see what was inside the storage unit, but Emma said they couldn't open it until Travis got there. "He gets weird about that sort of thing."

Marty knew better than to ask why. "Doesn't he have his own key?"

"He did, but he lost it," she said, shaking her head. "It's silly. This is mostly junk, stuff we got when we first got married. Even the furniture won't sell for much."

"Still, don't you deserve half of the profits?"

A slight blush touched her cheeks. "It's not a big deal. If he wants to go through the trouble of selling it, it's his. I feel bad that he lost his job."

Shoot. He knew that he should tell her it likely happened because of him, but that would open a whole can of worms. She might think he was crazy.

Maybe he was crazy. But at least he wasn't a jerk like Travis.

They ended up waiting a half hour longer. Marty didn't mind; he liked talking to Emma. The more time the better.

When Travis arrived and parked his shining BMW in the lot, Marty was ready. His muscles were tense but his mind was calm. He'd made up his mind that he wouldn't start any fights with Travis.

Not that Marty was a terribly confrontational guy, but he felt like Emma deserved someone who would stick up for her.

Travis got out of the car with a woman Marty assumed was Kimmy. She had a wide smile and big, blonde hair that bounced as she bounded toward them.

Travis plodded along behind her, his eyes fixed on his cell phone. He was different than Marty had imagined, dressed in ironed khakis and a tucked-in polo shirt.

For some reason, Marty expected him to be cool or suave or *something*. How this man managed to get not one, but two women to agree to marry him was beyond Marty.

"Hi," Emma said once they were closer.

Travis put his phone in his pocket and smiled. "Hey. Who's this?"

Marty stuck out a hand. "I'm Marty. Nice to meet you."

Travis nodded and shook his hand. "You didn't tell me you got a new boyfriend."

"He's not my boyfriend," Emma said, shooting a smile at Marty. "He's my friend."

Kimmy raised her eyebrows. "Cute friend."

If they were trying to make Marty feel unwelcome, it was working. He didn't care, though. He'd expected it, though perhaps in not such a passive-aggressive way.

"How are things? How's Dolto?" asked Emma.

Kimmy smiled. "Oh good. Everything's good. You look nice."

"Thanks. You do too!" Emma said.

Travis' two loves could not be more different. Emma had her dark hair in a low ponytail. Little wisps escaped around her face, giving her a casually beautiful glow. Marty wasn't sure if she was even wearing makeup. If she was, it was subtle.

Kimmy looked like she was going out on the town. She had tall heels and heavy makeup that made her eyes look huge. Her large diamond ring was pinched onto her manicured finger.

"Did you remember to bring the key?" asked Travis.

Emma nodded, pulling it from her pocket and handing it over.

"Thanks. Do you care if I sell that junk in there?"

Emma shrugged. "No, that's fine with me."

"Do you even want the key back?"

Emma thought on it for a second. "Maybe I could just take a look inside and make sure I didn't leave anything important?"

Travis nodded. "Okay."

He unlocked the unit and pulled open the clanking metal door. After turning on the light, he and Emma focused on walking through together and popping boxes open, speaking quietly about the contents.

Marty was left to entertain Kimmy, who seemed to have a permanent smile fixed on her ruby-red lips.

"So you're not her boyfriend?"

Marty shook his head. "I'm not. We work together."

"Really?" She dropped her voice. "You can tell me. Travis would be annoyed, but I don't care. I think it'd be good for her, honestly."

Marty shot a look over to Emma and Travis. They seemed to be out of earshot. "Why would Travis be annoyed?"

Kimmy shrugged and snapped her gum. "I don't know. He's like that. It's not personal or anything."

"Okay." Marty forced himself to smile. Kimmy seemed friendly enough. "But no, we're just friends. She's new on the island, and I've been showing her around."

"That's nice of you," Kimmy said, typing out a message on her phone. "Travis was so annoyed that she moved to that island. I thought I would never hear the end of it."

"Why?"

"You know," she waved a hand. "Stuff like this. It's a pain to see her or meet up with her."

Marty nodded. "Yeah, I get that." He didn't get it, but he was willing to play along. "I know she's been trying to visit Dolto for a while."

"Oh yeah?" Kimmy paused, suddenly unable to focus on her texting. "We should try to set that up."

There was something off in her response. Marty didn't know what it was, but he got a strange feeling in his chest. "Does Travis really like Dolto?"

"Yeah, I think so," Kimmy said with a shrug.

"How about you?"

Kimmy stopped what she was doing and looked up at him. "I mean, it's a cat. I'm not really a cat person."

Aha. So the line that Travis needed to keep Dolto for his doting fiancée was a lie. "I love cats."

"Yeah, they're cute." She was back to texting and snapping her gum.

Marty couldn't help himself. "I'd pay you for him."

"Oh yeah?" Kimmy laughed, still not moving her eyes from her phone. "How much?"

"It's negotiable," Marty said with a shrug. "I was thinking a thousand dollars."

Kimmy looked at him, mouth open. "Shut up."

"What?"

She slapped a hand onto his shoulder. "Seriously? You've got to be kidding."

"I'm dead serious." Marty stared her in the eye. "I'll give you a thousand dollars today, right now. Cash."

Kimmy bit her lip. "Travis! Get over here."

Marty's jaw tensed. He'd hoped he wouldn't have to involve Travis in this ill-planned scheme, but it seemed to be happening.

Whatever. He was ready.

Chapter Thirteen

"Your boyfriend is causing problems," Travis muttered under his breath.

Emma closed her eyes. She should have known it was a mistake coming here with Marty. "He's just a friend, I swear."

"Get over here!" Kimmy yelled.

Travis let out a sigh, dropping a box of old pots and pans and joining Kimmy near the entrance of the unit. Emma followed.

"What?" asked Travis.

"I found a way to get a thousand dollars for our wedding fund," Kimmy said with a smile.

Travis narrowed his eyes. "Really?"

"Marty wants to buy Dolto."

Emma looked at Marty, wide-eyed. "A *thousand* dollars?"

"I think it's a fair price," Marty said coolly.

A pang of terror hit Emma, going from her chest down through her feet. She thought Travis was going to yell, but unbelievably, he didn't.

Instead, he stood there and fidgeted. Could Marty be onto something?

Finally, Travis spoke. "I don't know, man. I don't think that's a good idea."

"Why not?" Marty crossed his arms. "Twelve hundred."

Kimmy smacked Travis in the shoulder. "We can get a new cat with twelve hundred dollars."

"It may not be that easy," he hissed.

Emma wanted to say something, but she couldn't. It felt like she was watching the conversation in slow motion.

Kimmy let a sigh. "We can figure it out. I'll figure it out."

Travis made a face. "Will you?"

"Yeah, I mean I love the cat," Kimmy said with a shrug. "Don't get me wrong, but he's expensive."

"Expensive?" asked Marty.

She nodded. "We had to take him to the emergency vet a few weeks ago for swallowing something. Luckily he didn't need surgery, but – "

Travis cut her off. "Do you have everything you need, Emma? Can we lock up? I have places to go."

She desperately wanted him to agree to Marty's terms, even though she didn't want Marty to spend that much money. She'd pay him back, though. She'd find a way. Emma just never thought Travis would go for something like that, or she would've tried it much sooner.

"Hello?" Travis said. "Earth to Emma. Can you hear me? It's mission control."

"No, I'm good," she said, forcing a smile. "You can have everything."

Travis nodded. "All right. Well, we really gotta get going."

They stepped out of the unit, and Travis pulled the door shut. Emma saw Marty take a card from his wallet and hand it to Kimmy. “Let’s talk,” he said quietly.

Kimmy winked at him and slipped it in her pocket. Travis didn’t seem to notice.

Emma had always thought Kimmy loved Dolto too much to give him up. That’s what Travis had told her, but now that seemed like a lie. Also…

Emma took a step toward Kimmy, getting the full force of her flowery perfume. “Did you say that Dolto didn’t need surgery?”

She nodded. “Mhm. Whatever he ate passed on its own. We got lucky, because that surgery would’ve been *so* expensive. And after Travis told off his boss – ”

Marty cut in. “You told off your boss?”

“I did, yeah. He deserved it.” Travis’ posture stiffened. “The whole vet stay was expensive, so don’t get any ideas, Emma.”

Before she could respond, Travis and Kimmy said their goodbyes and walked to their car.

Once they were gone, Marty turned to her. “What was that about?”

“I could ask you the same thing!” she said, hands on her hips. “You didn’t tell me you were going to offer to buy Dolto.”

“*I* didn’t know that I was going to offer to buy Dolto,” he said. “I swear. Kimmy was just…I don’t know. It seemed like it would work. I get ideas sometimes. I’m sorry.”

Emma let out a sigh. "It did seem like it might work. Travis always said Kimmy loved Dolto too much to give him up, but..."

"I know." Marty frowned. "I know you don't want to seem like a bitter ex-wife – I promise, you aren't that way in the least – but I think Travis might've made that up. Just to, I don't know, be mean to you."

Emma looked down at her shoes. "Maybe."

"I didn't know that Dolto needed surgery."

"Yeah." Emma bit on her nail. "Travis called me and said he'd lost his job and that Dolto was at the emergency vet. He said he needed two thousand dollars for surgery or Dolto might have to be put to sleep."

"What?"

Oh dear, Marty looked livid. "It's not a big deal. I'm sure the whole thing was expensive. It's just, well, he never told me that they ended up not doing the surgery. It's almost like..."

"He was trying to get money off you?" Marty suggested.

Emma shook her head. "There must be another reason."

Marty rubbed his face in his hands. "Emma, I'm sorry. This is going to be really hard for you to hear."

She braced herself, locking onto his beautiful green eyes. "Okay?"

"You're way too nice. Way, *way* too nice. I'm sure you've heard that before."

She laughed. "I might have."

"You can't give a guy like Travis the benefit of the doubt. He's just – I'm sorry, he's the worst. It's not your fault, but he is."

"He's not a bad person," Emma said. She heard how small her voice sounded, but she couldn't help it.

"If he wanted people to believe that, maybe he should stop doing bad things," Marty replied.

Emma nodded, but said nothing.

Marty softened his tone. "I'm sorry. I just think you need someone on your side. Travis has no problem looking out for himself. You deserve to have someone looking out for you, too."

She smiled. "Thanks for coming today. I'm sorry he was rude to you."

Marty laughed. "I don't care about that at all, but why should it bother him that I was here? He's engaged. He's starting a new life. Why can't he just let you live yours?"

"I don't know," she lied.

"Is he just the biggest jerk on Earth?"

Emma shook her head. "It's more complicated than that."

Marty squared his shoulders with hers. "How about we go to dinner and talk it over?"

She stared at him. He thought *she* was too nice? He was one to talk, putting up with all of this and driving her around!

"Please?" he added with a smile.

Emma couldn't help but smile back at him. "All right."

Traffic had died down, so they were able to get into the city and go to a restaurant near the SureFired office. Emma hadn't been there before, but Marty suggested it and he was spot on. The food was delicious and thankfully, it wasn't too expensive.

She wanted to pay her fair share, though, and it was nice that he gave in to her paying for the meal.

"Time to spill the beans," he said as they were finishing their last bites. "Is it fair to say that Travis is holding a grudge for some reason?"

She shrugged. "It's complicated."

"How?"

Emma had never talked about this, but somehow having Marty identify Travis' crummy behavior made her feel validated in a way. "When I got sick, it ruined his future."

"How did it ruin his future?" Marty asked softly.

"My sickness derailed our lives," she said. "I had to drop out of school, and I couldn't work. Travis had to pay all the bills. It was so stressful."

"I'm sure."

"At first, Travis was really sweet and supportive. He said he'd do anything that he needed to do to get me healthy. But it wore him down. Everyone felt bad for me because I was sick, but no one knew how much he was struggling."

Marty stared at her, but said nothing. She found herself unable to stop talking. "He always dreamt of having a big family with a lot of kids, and because of the transplant, there's a chance I may never be able to have kids safely."

He raised an eyebrow. "And?"

"I mean there's a chance, but – "

"No, not that," Marty said. "He's holding a grudge because your liver happened to fail and it made things a little bit harder for him?"

"That's not it exactly." She didn't know how to put it into words. She'd let Travis down. She'd forced him into a life he didn't want and couldn't handle. Even if she hadn't meant to. "Things were a lot harder."

"Isn't that why the vows say 'in sickness and in health?'" Marty reached across the table and gently touched her hand. "I'm sorry. I just think you're so... You're just great, and the fact that he would do that is cruel."

Marty had never touched her before. It happened so quickly, but it felt like her hand tingled long after he broke contact.

Emma offered him a weak smile. "It was hard for him, and he didn't want people to think less of him after we broke up."

Marty shook his head. "That's not your problem. The fact of the matter is that his wife, whom he was supposed to love and care for *in sickness and in health*, got sick, and all he could think about was himself."

Emma laughed. "You sound like my mom."

"She must be a smart woman." He leaned forward. "If he wanted people to think better of him, then he should have behaved better."

She took her last sip of water. "I know it's silly, but at the time I was so tired, and so confused and...I don't know. I felt so bad for what I'd done to our marriage. It felt like it was all my fault. My dad said I didn't try hard enough, that marriage means you have to put in extra work and...I don't know."

"It wasn't your fault," Marty said.

Emma laughed. "Still."

"It wasn't your fault," he said again.

His words hung in the air. Emma wanted to speak, but she didn't know what to say. Her dad was always telling her she was "too soft," and when her marriage failed, he said, "This is just another sign."

"Of what?" she'd asked.

He didn't even look at her when he answered. "Laziness."

That had hurt. It still hurt. While Travis never explicitly said it was her fault, but he would blame her for things – their finances, not being able to have kids, his deteriorating mental health...

Marty cleared his throat. "The thing about kids? You know I'm adopted, right? That is an option."

Emma laughed. "I know. He said that would be too expensive, though, and that we would never have any money because of me and all of the follow-up care I needed."

Marty choked on his water. "That's unreal. Listen. You can't let him keep punishing you for this." His voice was serious now. "You did nothing wrong. You did *nothing* wrong."

Emma felt like she was on the verge of tears, but she forced a smile and stood up from her seat. "Thanks, Marty."

"It's okay to admit that some people are selfish, or that they're acting selfishly. It doesn't mean you're being mean."

She nodded. "You're probably right. It's just hard for me."

"I know, and I'm sorry. I won't keep harping on this."

She shrugged. The tearful feeling passed. "Actually, it was nice to get this off my chest. I don't really talk about it, and when I hear myself say it out loud, I sound stupid."

"You do not sound stupid." He shook his head. "Not at all. It takes time to process a broken heart. You have to wade through the muddle to make sense of it all."

"That's a good way to put it." Emma smiled. Marty always found a way to make her feel better. "Do we have time to stop by your office?"

He looked at his watch. "I think so. I'll be quick."

Marty was right. Perhaps she'd given Travis the benefit of the doubt for too long. She'd felt so guilty about everything that she couldn't think straight.

Her dad still hadn't forgiven her for getting divorced. She'd been so full of shame, yet Marty didn't think she'd been in the wrong. He dismissed those voices in her head so easily. He made her feel so seen.

It was nice to have someone on her side.

Chapter Fourteen

Despite using the programs at the SureFired office, Marty wasn't able to trace the email from his so-called brother. He decided there was no harm in responding and asking the guy what his story was.

He wrote out his response quickly, hit send, and then he and Emma drove back to the Anacortes ferry terminal.

Marty hadn't told anyone about the email, but for some reason, when Emma had asked him what he'd needed to do at the office, he blabbed everything. He told her about the email and the strange letter he'd gotten months prior.

"Marty, this is crazy! What if you really do have a brother?"

He shrugged. "I don't know. It doesn't add up. If the guy wanted me to know who he was, why is he hiding himself so well?"

She smiled. "He's smart. Like you."

Her compliment kept Marty wide awake for the rest of the drive. They caught the last ferry of the night, and once they were back on Orcas, Marty drove to Emma's place to drop her off.

"I want to thank you for everything," Emma said as she opened the car door.

He waved a hand. "No, thank you. I honestly had a blast."

"Have a good night, Marty."

He watched to make sure that she got into her apartment safely before pulling away in a daze. Spending the day with her was simply amazing, and the drive had passed in no time. They hadn't even listened to music. They were too busy talking and laughing and having fun.

Seeing Travis wasn't as terrible as he'd expected. Also, now that he knew Travis had gotten himself fired from his job, Marty didn't feel so bad. His email interference might not have helped, but ultimately Travis seemed proud of what he'd done.

What an odd character. Marty tried his best to be understanding, but it felt impossible. Travis had abandoned his sick wife and then blamed her for her illness. Try as he might, he couldn't get into the mental space where Travis' actions made any sense.

Sure, it must've been hard, and it must've been stressful, but it seemed like Travis had taken his panic and fear and frustration and heaped it all onto Emma. It was an immature reaction, and Travis still saw himself as the victim.

Or perhaps it was more basic than that. Somewhere inside, maybe Travis knew he'd acted poorly. That deep shame and guilt could be eating away at him, but instead of facing it, he'd lashed out at Emma like a schoolchild.

At least Emma seemed like she was waking up to it. Travis had still managed to get a few thousand dollars off of her first. If Marty had known that, he would've offered even more for Dolto's return.

The money meant nothing to him. Since starting his new job, Marty's bank account continued to grow, but he'd spent almost nothing. The one luxury he'd allowed himself was a new set of headphones.

Poor Emma. Marty made up his mind. His mission was to get Dolto back for her. After all she'd been through, she deserved to be reunited with her beloved cat.

It seemed that his intuition about Kimmy was right. On Thursday morning, his phone rang with an unknown number. He answered it, hoping it was good news.

"Marty?" the voice asked. "It's Kimmy. I want to talk to about the cat."

Marty sat up. "I'm all ears."

"Okay, so, we have to make this deal without Travis knowing."

"That works for me."

She let out a sigh. "You can't get angry at me, either, because this isn't my fault."

He shifted in his chair. "Okay..."

"After Dolto got sick, Travis was really mad and said we needed to get rid of him."

Marty's heart rate was picking up. "Get rid of him? How?"

"Oh, not like that. Travis found someone and gave him away."

Marty noticed his breathing getting heavy. He reminded himself not to be angry with Kimmy. It wasn't her fault. Probably. "Who did you give him to?"

"That's the problem," Kimmy said. "Travis found a lady on Facebook. I messaged her a few times, but she hasn't answered me. I think she's ignoring me."

"Can you send me the person's profile?"

"Yeah!" She paused. "If you do find Dolto, though, do I still get the reward?"

Marty closed his eyes. "Yes. If I find Dolto, you'll get the reward."

"Like find him, as in the person confirms they have him?"

"No," Marty said. "I need to get Dolto."

She was quiet for a moment. "That's not really in my control."

Marty stayed silent, counting silently in his head.

When he reached seven, Kimmy spoke again. "Fine. I'll text you her name."

"Thanks, Kimmy. I'll be in touch."

Marty received her message a moment later and got to work. His first problem was that he didn't have a Facebook account. It would look suspicious if he messaged this person on an account with no friends and no pictures, so he threw something together.

He added a few people he knew, then uploaded a dozen pictures of himself and his hikes. He then sent a friend request to the woman who had allegedly picked up Dolto – a lady named Juno Marsh – and waited.

There wasn't much he could see from her profile, since it was marked private. It said that she lived in Yakima, Washington. Marty looked her up online and was able to find what he believed to be the woman's address.

That would be a last resort. He couldn't go knocking on doors like a madman. He didn't need the FBI coming after him again. No, he had to do this the hard way, with patience.

The hardest part of the process was deciding what to tell Emma. On one hand, her pleas might sway the mysterious Mrs. Marsh, who'd only had Dolto for a few days at most.

On the other hand, if it was some cruel trick by Kimmy, Marty didn't want to get Emma's hopes up. She'd suffered enough.

His goal was to show up at her door with Dolto in hand and end the nightmare that Travis had started.

It was his sole focus from now on.

Chapter Fifteen

It had been weeks and Claire still couldn't work up the courage to ask Marty about the letter she'd seen in his apartment. Her first instinct was to take Chip's advice and try to forget about it. She stayed busy at the hotel, and on top of that, she kept encouraging Chip to reconnect with his Lummi heritage.

He ultimately agreed, but only after he made Claire promise that they would attend the Lummi Nation Stommish Water Festival as anonymous guests. It was Chip's fear that he'd run into someone he used to know from his visits to the reservation as a boy; in his head, the person would be angry that Chip had been gone for so long and they would reject him.

Claire thought that was unlikely, but it had taken months for her to convince him that no one would be angry with him, and even further, that it was unlikely anyone would recognize him.

So they went for the music, and the canoe races, and the food, and within an hour, Chip was carrying on and laughing with a gaggle of new friends. He ended up running into someone he'd known as a teen. However, the man didn't shun him – he literally welcomed Chip with open arms, wrapping him in a huge bear hug.

They returned to Orcas with Chip's spirits buoyed. Claire was so happy for him. He was overjoyed to be back. His fears had been unfounded, and he was already planning his next trip.

Disappointingly for Claire, this meant she had more time to be preoccupied with that letter.

Margie was convinced that talking to Marty was the only way to figure anything out. "Otherwise," she argued, "you'll come up with all kinds of crazy stories in your head!"

Claire knew Margie was right, but she couldn't bring herself to do it. Marty was a private person, more so than almost anyone else she knew. Unlike Lucy, who was an open book, Marty liked to keep things to himself. He was shy, in a way.

If she started asking questions or sticking her nose where it shouldn't be, he might pull away. She might offend him, or he might think she was losing it, clinging to the hope that Becca might still be alive.

For the most part, Claire kept these thoughts to herself. Except when she spent time with Margie.

Today was such a day. Margie had heard about a new tea shop on Orcas that offered high tea, and they made an early reservation and went off like a pair of giddy school girls.

The tea was lovely, with delicate cucumber sandwiches, enormous blueberry scones served with clotted cream, and dessert chocolates. It was fun catching up with Margie, and best of all, Margie was always up for brainstorming. On the drive back to the hotel, she presented her new ideas on the letter.

"Can you invite yourself over and pretend to find it again?" asked Margie.

Claire laughed. "I don't think I'm good enough of an actress to pull that off."

"That's a shame." Margie tapped her chin. "What if we both went over?"

"I don't know. Even thinking about it makes me feel queasy."

Margie motioned to something ahead on the road. "Watch out. There's a broken-down car up there."

"I see it," Claire said with a nod. She slowed down as they passed, only to realize a moment too late that the person standing next to the car was Emma.

"Shoot!" Claire said, looking for a place to turn around. "That's one of my employees."

"Which one? Was it Gigi?" Margie asked. "She keeps calling me Barbie. I think she does it to annoy me, and it's working."

"No, it was Emma, who I think will be able to remember your name."

Margie dropped her voice to a whisper. "The one that Marty likes?"

Claire shot her a look. "Not a *word!* I mean it, Margie!"

Margie giggled and pretended to zip her lips. "You won't hear a peep out of me."

Claire pulled over and both she and Margie got out of the car.

"Hey! Is everything okay?" asked Claire.

"Hi!" Emma walked toward them, her face twisted into a frown. "I'm not late yet, am I? My car broke down. I think it's overheating? I'm not really sure."

A plume of steam billowed from under the hood. Claire was no car expert, but she'd broken down many times on the side of the road. "Looks like it. Do you want me to call a tow truck?"

Emma bit her lip. "You don't think it'll cool down and I can get back in?"

Margie made a face. "That doesn't seem safe. We can give you a ride."

Claire nodded. "I'll talk to Chip. I'm sure he knows the best mechanics on the island. Just hang on a second."

She stepped aside as she made the call. Luckily Chip answered, and he knew exactly who to send Emma to – a guy named Jim who had a garage and tow truck not far from where Emma had broken down. He said he'd give him a call and ask him to head over.

When Claire rejoined Emma and Margie, she realized there was a fourth person in the mix. A red-faced man was wildly pointing at the car, at Emma, and at Margie.

Claire rushed over to see what the problem was.

"Get that hunk of junk out of here *now!*" he yelled. "This is private property!"

"I'm sorry, I'm going to move it as soon as I can, but – " Emma stammered, her voice small.

"I don't care! You're killing my grass!" the man said, little spit balls forming on his lips.

Claire was about to speak when Margie beat her to it. "Listen here, buddy. She didn't pick your lawn to break down on purpose. We'll get the car out of here when we feel like it. If you keep throwing a fit, maybe we'll even stay overnight."

"I'll have it towed to the junkyard," he said, thrusting his face inches from Margie's.

Margie was undeterred. "Oh yeah? I'd like to see you try!"

"I'll call the police," he said in a low growl, narrowing his eyes.

Margie scoffed. "Great! You're just going to end up on the phone with my husband."

The man stared at her, as though trying to figure out if she was bluffing.

Claire stepped in. "The tow truck is on its way. We'll be out of here soon."

The man shot her a look before turning back to Emma. "You'd better pay for the grass that you killed, too."

"We certainly will not," Margie said, pointing a finger in his face, causing him to take a step back. "The ground isn't soft, and there's no damage at all. It's crabgrass anyway. I have half a mind to – "

"Okay. Let's all just cool down," Claire interrupted. "It's hot out. Emma and Margie, let's go sit in my car until the tow truck gets here."

Margie shot the man one last menacing look before following Claire to the car.

Once they were safely locked inside, Emma spoke again. "I'm so sorry that you got dragged into this. I didn't want to pull onto the grass. The only other option was to stay in the middle of the road, and with the way the road curves I was worried I would get hit."

"You did the right thing," Margie said. "That man is just a grump. And rude! I'm going to come back here late at night and kill the rest of his crabgrass."

Claire laughed. "I don't think that would help us in this situation, Margie, but I do admire your spirit."

Margie let out a huff. Her cheeks were pink. "I'm sorry. I got a little carried away there. I just can't stand it when people are so *rude.*"

Emma smiled. "Thank you for that. He started getting so angry and I didn't know what to do."

Margie reached back and patted her on the shoulder. "You're young still. Believe it or not, there are some benefits to getting older. I picked up a lot of skills along the way, like how to deal with an idiot."

"I need to pick up some skills," Emma said with a small laugh.

Claire felt so bad for her in that moment. She was a sweet girl, and she didn't seem to have a mean bone in her body. "Don't worry. I'm sure you'll pick up a lot of skills working in customer service," Claire said. "Though I hope our guests aren't being mean to you."

"Oh no, almost everyone is nice." Emma smiled. "When they're not, it doesn't bother me much."

"No wonder everyone likes you," Margie said.

Claire shot her a look. Margie was getting ready to make comments, she could just feel it. Claire regretted telling her about Marty's crush on Emma.

She decided to change the topic. "Emma, I spoke to Chip and he has a friend who owns a car shop on the island. He'll be the one coming to pick up your car."

Emma nodded. "Thank you."

Jim showed up after about twenty minutes and was as nice as could be. He promised that he'd take a look at Emma's car that day, and that he might have it back to her within a few days.

"Hm," Claire said as they drove off. "You don't have access to another car, do you?"

Emma shook her head. "I don't."

"I'm sure Marty would be happy to drive you wherever you need to go," Margie said.

Just like that. It just took one instant with Margie. She couldn't be stopped.

"I would hate to ask that of him," Emma said.

"He wouldn't mind. He's the nicest guy, isn't he, Claire? The nicest guy."

Claire kept her eyes on the road. She couldn't bear to look at Margie. "He is."

"We can call him and ask him," Margie continued. "Or maybe he's at the hotel now?"

Emma cleared her throat. "No. He's done far too much for me already. I wouldn't want to ask that of him."

"Maybe Jim will fix your car today," Claire offered.

"He probably won't be able to," Margie countered. "Marty's always looking for something to do anyway. He loves driving."

There was no stopping her. Claire clenched her teeth and tried not to make the situation worse.

They got to the hotel and, as expected, Marty was in the office working away. Claire tried to leave Margie behind, but she was on a roll.

"Emma's car broke down on the way to work today," Claire said as she walked into the office.

"Oh no." Marty looked genuinely alarmed. "Is she okay?"

Claire nodded. "Yes, she's fine. We gave her a ride and helped her get her car to a shop."

"Now she doesn't know how she's going to get to work every day, though," Margie added. "I suggested that maybe you could drive her, because I know the two of you are friends."

Marty's eyes darted between them. "We are."

"It seems like Emma was worried that you've done too much for her, though," Margie continued. "What have you been doing for her?"

Claire glared at her. "Margie, I don't think it's any of our business, do you?"

Marty laughed. "It's okay. I haven't done much, I don't think. I gave her a ride to the mainland a few days ago, and I've been trying to help get her cat back."

Margie crossed her arms. "Get her cat back from where?"

"Her ex-husband."

Margie walked over to him and started fussing, first pulling a fleck of something off of his shoulder, then petting his hair. "Well, if that's not the sweetest thing I've ever heard! Why don't you go out there and tell her the good news that you'd be happy to drive her wherever she needs to go?"

"Sure. I don't mind."

"Good!" Margie said.

"Why do I feel like you're about to pinch my cheeks?" Marty asked with a half-smile.

"I'll pinch your ears if you don't get out there and talk to her soon," Margie said.

Marty jumped from his desk and Claire mouthed an "I'm sorry," as he passed by.

He laughed and shook his head, walking out the door.

Once he was safely out of earshot, Claire turned to her friend. "Hey Margie?"

"Yes?"

Claire crossed her arms. "Have you ever thought of picking up the skill of subtlety?"

"I did, but I decided it's not for me," she said with a laugh.

Chapter Sixteen

His main goal had been to get away from Margie, but once in the hallway, Marty hesitated. Why was she so insistent on him driving Emma? Did Margie know how he felt? Was he that obvious?

No. She couldn't have known. That's just how Margie was, ever playing the matchmaker. She'd given Claire a hard time for years. It must've been a relief when Chip had come around.

Marty wasn't going to read too much into it.

He made his way to the front desk, but once he got there, he felt sheepish and didn't know what to say.

Emma popped up from behind the counter. "Hey!"

"Hi," he said. "I heard you had some car trouble?"

Emma winced. "Yeah. My car broke down, then Claire found me, which was super embarrassing."

"Don't be embarrassed," Marty said. He paused. "Margie mentioned that you may not have a car for a few days?"

Emma's cheeks flushed. "Yes, but don't worry about it. She tried to volunteer you to drive me, but I would never ask that of you."

Excellent. She'd brought it up. That made it easy. "I don't mind."

"No, it's really okay," Emma said, shaking her head.

There wasn't even public transportation on the island; she would really be out of luck. Emma seemed so flustered, too. It made Marty feel awful.

He needed to be more convincing. Marty leaned forward and dropped his voice. "To be honest, she kind of came into the office and threatened me, so I'm pretty sure if you don't let me drive you around, something bad is going to happen to me."

Emma's eyes widened. "I'm so sorry."

"Don't be. That's just Margie. She believes in neighbors helping neighbors." He smiled. "Plus, I know what it's like to have an old car. I don't mind at all. So please, just text me your schedule before Margie comes after me."

Emma stared at him for a beat before responding. "Are you sure?"

"Positive," he said with a nod. "You're doing me a favor."

She pursed her lips. "Oh, stop. Hopefully it won't be for long, maybe just a couple of days. Margie really pushes for what she wants, doesn't she?"

"Yeah." Marty sighed. "You could say that."

"She and Claire were a huge help today."

Marty shrugged. "That's what friends are for."

Emma smiled. *Finally!*

A moment later, someone stepped up behind Marty. Since they were a real customer, he had to get out of the way.

"Let me know when you're done today."

She nodded. "Thanks, Marty."

When he got back to the office, Claire was busy talking to Chip, but Margie was waiting for him.

"Marty, I wanted to tell you – "

He held up a hand. "Margie, don't worry. I will be driving Emma wherever she needs to go until her car is fixed."

She smiled broadly. "That's nice. I was just going to say it was lovely running into you today."

Claire shot him an apologetic look and he laughed. "You too, Margie."

Claire and Margie left soon after, and Marty got back to pretending to do work. Unfortunately for him, Emma skipped her lunch break, citing her late arrival to work. He didn't get to see her again until he drove her home that evening. It was short, but pleasant.

Marty decided to get creative to maximize his time with her. For the rest of the week, he made sure to create playlists so they didn't have to suffer through radio ads. He kept the car the perfect temperature and made sure his tank was at least half full.

One morning, he got them both coffee. This was a risky move. On the one hand, it could look like he was trying too hard, but on the other hand, Emma loved it. The first time he had a coffee waiting for her, she was so delighted that he didn't dare stop buying them.

There was an immature part of him that hoped her car would never be fixed, but sadly, on Friday evening, she got the call that all was well. Marty dropped her off at the repair shop early Saturday morning and set his mind to finding new ways to spend time with her.

The timing of Emma's repair couldn't have been better, however. When he got back home and logged onto his computer, Marty saw that he'd received another email from his so-called brother.

The message didn't say much. His mysterious half-brother ignored his suggestion about meeting up, and instead reiterated how wild it was that they were related. The message was littered with typos, and this time, the sender did not disguise his location. Marty was able to trace it to a house in the suburbs of Seattle.

Marty swung by the hotel to tell Emma about the email and his plan to surprise the sender.

"I don't know if that's a good idea, Marty," Emma said, her voice almost a whisper.

"Why not? I want to see if he looks like me."

She frowned. "What if he's violent or something?"

"Why would he be violent?"

"I don't know," she said, eyes wide. "Because people are sometimes!"

Marty waved a hand. "I'm just going to stop by and check it out. Don't worry. I won't talk to him if he looks dangerous."

He was able to catch the next ferry and didn't hit any traffic on his drive down. When he got to the house, he parked outside and debated what to do. Emma was right. He couldn't just knock on the door and introduce himself.

Suddenly he was missing the bravado he'd had in front of her. What if this guy was a liar? What if he had some sort of ulterior motive?

Marty had gotten a decent amount of wacky letters since the FBI had given him his fifteen minutes of fame, but this was the only person he'd taken seriously.

Partially, this was because of his own curiosity. The emailer was the only one who'd contacted him claiming to be a relative. He knew a lot about Marty and his past. They knew about his biological mother and the plane crash. That had to mean something.

Marty sat there for half an hour, chewing this over in his mind, when the front door to the house opened. A guy came out, but Marty couldn't see his face. He leaned forward, watching until the guy turned around.

As soon as Marty saw him, the excitement in his chest died. It wasn't his half-brother. It was no one special at all, just his least favorite coworker, David Monroe.

Marty got out of the car, practically running up to David.

"Hey!" he yelled.

David looked surprised to see him. He also stunk of alcohol. "Hey man. What's up?"

Marty stared at him. "When were you going to tell me that you were my brother?"

"What? I have no idea what you're talking about," David said.

Marty was unconvinced. "I traced your email."

"You traced my email?" David crossed his arms and fidgeted. "It was just a joke, man. Lighten up."

The "just a joke" defense. Used by every person who'd ever crossed a boundary and refused to apologize.

Clearly, David's jealousy over Marty's promotion hadn't passed. Marty thought the snide comments he'd made at the office would be the end of it, but no. David had to take it a step further. He had crossed a line.

It didn't matter, though. Marty wasn't going to let David get to him. He wasn't even angry. He shook his head and let out a sigh. "You're pathetic."

Marty turned and walked back to his car. As he opened the door, David yelled from the sidewalk.

"You're not going to make a big deal about this at work, are you?"

Marty ignored him and got back in his car.

As he drove back to Anacortes, he worked through his thoughts. In truth, when he was alone, he was able to admit that he was disappointed. Even though he thought it was fake from the beginning, there was still some small part of him that had hoped it was real.

He was embarrassed by this, and ashamed of himself for some reason. Maybe because he should've known better.

He was gullible. That wasn't his only fault. The longer he drove, the more he beat himself up.

Gullible was the least of his problems. Who cared if David had tricked him? At least he managed to confront him in the end. Outside of this situation, though, Marty was a coward. He knew that, and that's what bothered him most.

He'd actually hoped that Emma's car wouldn't be repaired so she would be forced to see him every day. What kind of a jerk hopes for someone's car to be totaled?

A stand-up guy like Marty. He was so afraid to lay out how he felt that instead he followed her around like a puppy, making excuses to see her.

How long was he going to keep that up?

It was pathetic. It wasn't that he'd never asked her out. He did, all the time. He'd ask her to go to dinner, or go hiking, or go to an event on the island. She always said no.

He told himself she was just busy, and that was true. Yet it was clear she thought of him as a *friend.* She'd even say things like, "You're such a great friend. Thanks for the ride," and "It's so nice to have friends on the island."

It killed him. He couldn't bring himself to keep asking her out because it seemed like it was Emma's subtle, kind way of warning him not to hope for more.

If he actually told her how he felt, it would be over. She'd have to officially tell him no. They'd both be upset and things would get awkward. It was too much for him to face.

He couldn't go on like this, though. He was being a coward. He was acting like David or something, creeping around, unable to express himself like an adult.

Well, maybe he wasn't as bad as David. He wasn't a bitter, petty little man. He was just... awkward. Afraid. Emma held his heart in her hands, and it seemed like she had no idea.

He needed to tell her how he felt. Soon.

But not yet. As he pulled onto the ferry, he told himself he'd wait just a *bit* longer before making a move. He needed to get Dolto back. Not so Emma would fall in love with him, but because if he ruined their friendship with his feelings, it'd be harder for them to work together on getting the cat back. Once that was done, he would come clean.

Yeah. After Dolto. That was a good timeline. He still had some time.

Chapter Seventeen

Waiting to hear from Marty made the day drag. Emma was worried about him, and after a few hours, she finally got a message: "False alarm, no brother. He wasn't violent, either. I'll explain later."

She frowned. It didn't sound good, but at least he hadn't been hurt. She let out a sigh of relief and put her phone away.

Addie noticed this dramatic display and leaned in. "Is everything okay?"

Emma nodded. "Everything's fine. Why?"

"Trouble in paradise with you and Marty?"

"We're just friends," Emma said with a laugh. "So no."

The phone rang and Addie jumped to grab it. Emma stood next to her, feeling slightly jittery. She wasn't sure what it was. Addie's teasing didn't bother her. That was nothing.

It was more how worried she'd been about Marty. At first, she had been worried whoever sent that email might hurt him. Now, she was worried that person did hurt him, just not physically.

When Addie got off the phone, she turned to Emma with a grin. "Hang on. I brought something for you."

Emma waited until she returned from the break room with a folded newspaper. "Look at this. The front page story."

Emma unfolded the paper to find a picture of Marty in black and white. Her heart fluttered. Next to him was Blaise, both of them posed under the snappy headline "SureFired's CEO is Sure of One Thing: Success."

She skimmed the article quickly. It was mainly an interview where Blaise talked about his excitement for the SureFired technology. He also gushed about his staff.

That was where Marty came in. According to Blaise, Marty was "a beacon of integrity, refusing to back down even with the FBI on his tail."

"Oh my," Emma said quietly.

"I figured you'd want to have a copy." Addie giggled. "Marty's turning into quite a celebrity."

"Looks like it," Emma said, staring at his picture. He looked so cool. "Are you sure I can keep this?"

Addie nodded. "Definitely. It's kinda old, actually. My Gran saved it for me because it mentions the hotel. I thought you'd get a kick out of it."

Emma smiled. "Thanks." It would be fun to show Marty later. It might even cheer him up.

Addie finished her shift and left for the day, and Emma was left to fend for herself for a few hours until Gigi arrived. It was busy, but manageable, and the time flew by.

Gigi arrived in sour spirits, as usual, but Emma didn't mind. She was relieved to have a break for the evening; she'd worked double shifts the last three days at the daycare because one of her coworkers had been sick. All she wanted to do was eat a microwaved baked potato and go to sleep.

She was about to leave when Dan, one of the servers from The Plum Spoon, stopped by.

"Do you have plans tonight?" he asked.

Emma shrugged. "Just going home. I'm pretty tired. Why?"

"The chef wants to try out a new special. I thought you might like a free dinner."

"Oh." She wasn't one to turn down a delicious meal, but she felt so tired.

"You can bring a friend, if you want," he suggested.

That would definitely cheer Marty up. "Actually, that'd be great!"

Dan smiled. "Awesome. Let me know what time and I'll save a table for you."

"Thanks, Dan," Emma said.

Gigi was clearly not impressed by this interaction, and since Emma had ignored her sighs, she spoke up. "How come you get all the free stuff? Is it because you flirt with everyone?"

Emma looked up from the text she'd been typing out to Marty. "I don't flirt with everyone."

"Yeah, okay." She rolled her eyes. "I've never seen a girl so desperate for a boyfriend in my life. You need to chill."

What had gotten into Gigi? She was usually mean, but in a passive way. Emma didn't know how to address her, so instead she turned back to her phone.

She was about to hit send when, to her surprise, Marty appeared at the receptionist desk.

"Oh! I was just texting you," she said.

"Really? I must've sensed it."

Gigi scoffed. Emma refused to look at her. She cleared her throat and focused on Marty. "Dan just told me that the chef at The Plum Spoon wants to try out a new meal and is looking for guinea pigs. Are you up for it?"

Marty looked tired even as he smiled. "Yeah, that sounds good."

"I'm pretty sure he was trying to hit on you," Gigi interjected. "I don't think he wanted you to bring another guy."

Emma eyed her wearily. "He wasn't trying to hit on me."

Gigi raised her eyebrows. "Are you serious? You know, if you're trying that hard to fish for a boyfriend – "

"I'm not fishing for a boyfriend," Emma said firmly. "I'm not looking to date anyone."

"Maybe you should let Dan know before you take that free meal," Gigi said with a tight smile.

Marty cleared his throat. "Dan's not interested in women."

"What?" Gigi cocked her head to the side. "Really?"

Marty nodded. "Yeah. So your theory falls apart."

The look on Gigi's face was priceless. Emma had to force herself not to laugh. She waved goodbye, walking to the restaurant side by side with Marty.

Chapter Eighteen

Dan caught sight of them right away and gave them a seat out on the patio. The warm day had now turned to a pleasantly cool evening.

Dan told them about the special – a halibut cake with beet hummus and braised pork belly – and promised to return shortly with their drinks.

"Is that true? About Dan?" asked Emma.

Marty nodded. "Yeah. I didn't make it up. I think Gigi has a crush on him."

"*Oh!*" Emma shook her head. "I was wondering why she was being so especially mean."

Marty shrugged. "That's just Gigi."

It was hard for him to focus on what she was saying. Try as he might, he couldn't stop Emma's words from echoing in his mind. *I'm not looking to date anyone.*

She could've said she wasn't interested in Dan, but instead, she said she wasn't interested in anyone.

Including him.

Emma seemed to notice his silence. "What happened today? You seem down."

"Everything's fine, it's just..." He let out a sigh. It would be impossible to keep spending time with her now if that was how she felt. He wasn't simply interested in being her friend. It would be dishonest to pretend. Even now, sitting across from her made him feel physically ill.

"Did you meet him? Your mystery brother?"

He nodded. "I did."

"And?"

Marty leaned back. He needed to pull it together. He managed to tell her about driving to the house, seeing David, and confronting him.

"I'm so sorry, Marty," Emma said. "That's an incredibly cruel trick. Why would he do that?"

"Who knows." Marty shrugged. "He's always been a jerk, but after I got promoted, it got worse. He thought he deserved the promotion more. Told everyone about it."

"He's a sore loser," Emma said.

Marty stared at her. She looked so pretty. Even after working all day, she had a sort of glow. "Must be."

Their meals arrived and though they looked delicious, Marty had no appetite. He took a few bites, mainly so he could talk to Emma about the flavors. It was better than talking about his lame self.

He was halfway through eating his meal when, out of nowhere, he heard the sound of a slap. An envelope appeared on the table in front of him.

"Thanks for not going through the mail during your shift," Gigi said, arms crossed.

"I'm sorry," Emma stammered. "I thought Addie did it this morning."

Gigi let out a dramatic sigh. "She didn't, so both of you left the work to me. Thanks."

She walked off and Marty leaned forward. "Looks like she's still mad."

"She hates working the night shift," Emma said, shaking her head. "She said it's unfair that I don't work nights, too."

"How could you? You have another full-time job." Marty rolled his eyes. "She's always unhappy. She'll get over it."

Emma nodded toward the letter. "What's that?"

"Not sure," he said. Marty ripped the envelope open and pulled out the sheet of paper inside. It was handwritten, like the one he'd gotten months prior.

Dear Marty,

I saw the article about you in the paper. I'm so proud of you. I think it's safe to say you don't take after me. Ha! Keep up the good work.

- B

Marty read the letter to himself first, then aloud.

"What do you think that's about?" asked Emma.

Marty shook his head. "I have no idea. If this is David, I'm going to go back to his house and – "

Emma held up a hand. "Do you really think David would write a letter like that?"

"Maybe. He seemed to think it was really fun to mess with me before."

Dan stopped by to ask how they liked their meals, and they took a moment to share feedback. There wasn't much to say since it was delicious, though Marty commented that he could do with more beet.

Once Dan left, Marty tucked the letter into his pocket. "I don't want to think about this right now. There are too many weirdos who see me on the news or in the paper and get ideas. What's new with you?"

Emma shrugged. "Nothing. Just working. Can you believe I'm going to have to drive *myself* home from work today?"

Marty laughed. "The horror."

The restaurant was busy, so as soon as they were finished, they thanked Dan and headed to their cars. Marty wished Emma a safe drive home and retreated to his apartment to think.

It was too much. David's emails were cruel, but that wasn't the real reason he was upset. It all had to do with Emma.

Of course she wasn't looking for a boyfriend. Why would she be? She had so much going on in her life. She'd just gotten through her illness, then immediately went through a divorce and a move.

Even still, Marty was angry with himself. Deep down, he knew she never had any romantic feelings toward him. He'd just hoped it would change.

It wasn't that he didn't value her friendship, because he did. He'd be lucky to have a friend like her. It was silly that he'd expected more, hoped for more.

Hoping always got him into trouble.

Marty made up his mind. From then on, there would be no more hopes and no more schemes.

He then did the only thing that seemed reasonable: he stayed up far too late watching *Schitt's Creek.*

The next morning, Marty awoke from his restless sleep with a phone call. He did a double take when he saw Lucy's name on his phone.

"Hello?"

"Sounding a little groggy there, Marty," she said cheerfully. "Is everything okay?"

He yawned. "Yeah. What's up?"

"Well, I'm on my way to Claire's house to surprise her."

"Surprise her?" He sat up and rubbed his eyes. "You're on the island?"

"That's right! I'm going to pick up some stuff from the bakery, so I expect to see you at Claire's, too."

It would be nice to see Lucy again. "You had me at bakery."

Lucy laughed. "Good. See you soon!"

It was just as well; he had no other plans for the day. He still hadn't heard back from Juno, the woman who allegedly had Dolto, and he needed something to distract him from thinking about Emma.

He got ready quickly, and when he realized that the letter was still in his coat pocket from the night before, he decided to keep it there. Against his better judgment, he also grabbed the first letter. Lucy might have some ideas, and he figured it was time to tell Claire, too.

When he arrived at Claire's house, the scene was all excitement and cheer. Claire had had no idea Lucy was coming to visit. As he listened to Lucy talk, Marty got the idea that she hadn't planned it either.

"How does your work feel about this impromptu trip?" Marty asked with a smile.

Lucy glared at him. "Why? What do you know?"

He stifled a laugh. He didn't know much, just that Lucy started the new job at the same time she started hinting she had "hot dates" planned. He'd assumed she started dating a coworker. "Nothing, though your reaction tells me something."

"Fine." Lucy crossed her arms. "I also happened to quit my job. But that's not the only reason I came!"

Marty laughed. "I didn't mean to make you spill the beans."

"There are no beans to spill," Lucy said with a sigh. "That's just what happened. No big deal."

"What about the guy you were seeing, Lucy?" asked Claire.

Lucy made a face. "That's over, too."

"I'm sorry, honey," Claire said.

"It's fine!" Lucy said brightly. "It's all fine!"

Marty stared at her for a second. There was more to that story, but he wouldn't press her right now. He decided to change the topic. "I'm glad you're here. I wanted your advice on something."

A smile spread across Lucy's face. "Oh really? What is it? Girl troubles?"

"No." He cracked a pastry in two and stuffed a piece into his mouth. "It's a long story, but I don't want to bore you guys."

"You could never bore us, Marty," Claire said. "What's going on?"

He finished one pastry as he told the story of David and his emails. Then, he started on a donut. Stress eating wasn't one of his most charming qualities, but it worked in a pinch.

"I told you we should've taught David a lesson when we had the chance," Lucy said, eyes narrowed.

Marty loved having Lucy on his side; she was like an attack dog. "That's not the whole story. There's also these."

He pulled the letters out of his jacket and handed one to each of them. "Claire, I got that letter a few months ago. That was the first one. The one you have, Lucy? I just got yesterday."

Now he had their attention. They swapped letters, pointing at the signature and buzzing with ideas.

"Do you think this was David, too?" asked Lucy. "Just tell me where he lives. I'll get it out of him."

He shook his head. "I'm not sure. I was going to ask him, but it would be odd for him to do both, wouldn't it?"

Claire was frowning deeply, but said nothing.

"What do you think, Claire?" he asked.

She looked up at him, biting her lip. "I don't know what to think."

"The first letter is whatever," Lucy said. "Nonspecific. But that second letter sounds like it was written by a relative, at least to me. It looks like the postmarks are from Oregon. Do you know anyone in Oregon? Did you ever figure out who your biological dad was, Marty?"

He shook his head. "No. I figured he probably didn't even know I existed."

"That might be true," Lucy said with a frown. "Sorry, man."

Marty shrugged. "It's okay. It doesn't bother me. Honestly. I just don't know why someone would want to play this trick on me twice."

"That would be so cruel," Claire said. She was still staring at the letters.

Lucy leaned in. "Could it be Marty's long-lost dad? Or is it Becca from the grave?"

Claire flashed a faint smile. "I have no idea, but it's very strange."

Lucy groaned. "Marty, can't you track these letters down somehow? Scan them into the system, trace the paper or something?"

Marty laughed. "I don't work in a forensic lab. I could barely trace those emails back to David. There's no useful information on these letters at all."

"Dust them for fingerprints!" Lucy said, her mouth popping open.

Claire shook her head. "You watch too much TV. Besides, all of our fingerprints are on them now."

Lucy shrieked and dropped the letter in her hands. "You're right! No one touch them. I'll find gloves."

Marty buried his head in his hands. She was too much. "We're not dusting for fingerprints. I just wanted to get your opinion on them. There's not much I can do unless this person decides to reveal who they are."

Lucy pouted. "You give up too easily."

"If only that were true," Marty said with a sigh. When Lucy shot him a puzzled look, he cleared his throat. "I'll update you later."

Claire stared at him for a moment before turning to Lucy. "Should I understand that you're moving in with me?"

Lucy smiled. "If you don't mind?"

Claire hugged her. "I would love it. We're going to have so much fun!"

Marty smiled. He felt better, even though nothing was resolved. The fact that he wasn't totally alone meant something – perhaps everything.

Chapter Nineteen

Since Claire had to work for the rest the day, Lucy was left to hang out with Marty. She was glad to see him. She'd missed him ever since she'd left the island, though they had stayed in touch.

Marty was pretty good about keeping her up to date on the happenings at the hotel. He seemed different now, though. He seemed sad.

"Are these letters really messing with you?" she asked.

He shrugged. "Not really. What David did was scummy, but that's him."

"We need to get back at him," Lucy said firmly. "Are you busy today? Or do you have time to brainstorm revenge?"

He shook his head. "There's no need for revenge. I still have to work with the guy. It's not a big deal."

"It *is* a big deal!" Lucy said, staring him down. "It's obvious that it's upsetting you."

He was quiet for a moment before responding. "It's not that."

"Then what is it?"

He shrugged. "I don't know."

Lucy took a seat on the couch and let out a huff. "You're not being very forthcoming, so I'm going to have to start snooping and you're not going to like it."

He sat down too. "It's nothing."

"What is it?" She leaned forward. "Are you having girl troubles?"

He glanced at her, then back down at the ground. "I guess."

Oh, poor Marty. Lucy knew she needed to handle this with tact. Unfortunately, tact wasn't one of her strengths. "Do you want to talk about it?"

"Not really, but thanks."

Shoot. That didn't work. Maybe she should start with an embarrassing story of her own. "I'll tell you why I had to quit my job."

"Did something happen?"

"You could say that," Lucy said, tapping her chin. "I kinda sorta started dating my boss."

Marty's face broke into a smile. "You're kidding."

"I wish I was. It was a really dumb thing to do. We went on a couple of dates. He seemed so cool."

Marty narrowed his eyes. "He was your hot date, wasn't he?"

"Yeah," she said with a wistful sigh. It had been so romantic at first. "I started out really liking him, but with each date, I liked him less and less."

Marty hid his face behind his hands. "Stop. I can't take it. I'm feeling too much secondhand embarrassment for you."

"Okay, but I actually had to *live* it. How do you think I feel?" She choked on a laugh. This was not one of her finest moments, but she was hoping it would help Marty feel better. "At first, he seemed mysterious yet straightforward. It turns out, though, that he's just rude and boorish. He has a history of dating employees that work beneath him, too, which I didn't know."

"Ah." Marty nodded. "He's a predator."

Lucy shook her head. "No, he's not even that skilled. As soon as I told him I thought we were better off as friends, it got so awkward at work. He couldn't look me in the eye. If he saw me walking in the hall, he'd dart into the nearest room. He fell into a bucket in the closet once."

"You shouldn't have to quit because of that. He should be mature enough to get over it."

"I didn't like the job anyway," she said, waving a hand. "The pay was good, though, so I've got some savings until I can figure out my next steps."

"If you need any money, I'm happy to help."

"Ew," Lucy pulled back. "Don't flash your fancy salary at me!"

"I don't – I mean, I just want to be helpful." Marty laughed. "That's the funny thing. I've never had money before, and now that I do, the people that I actually care about and want to help won't accept a penny from me."

Lucy shrugged. "I'm too proud. I make my money the old-fashioned way." She paused. "By dating my boss."

They both laughed at that.

Marty didn't bring up his girl troubles again, and Lucy didn't ask. Instead, she suggested they go for a hike. Marty was the expert on these things, and he promised something that Lucy could enjoy.

It ended up being a trail in Moran State Park. Though Lucy liked to work out, hiking wasn't always her favorite activity. The bugs and mud got to her.

They hiked a trail that went by Cascade Falls. It was a series of waterfalls, the tallest being forty feet. Thankfully, there wasn't any mud at all. In fact, the trail was quite dusty.

Despite the mess, Lucy decided it was worth it. There were nice flowers and trees, and it seemed plunging into all that nature improved Marty's mood. He stood and stared at the waterfall for five minutes, not saying a word.

Lucy was enjoying herself, too, until she heard the screams of someone who'd gotten pooped on by a bird. After that, she was ready to leave.

They were going to go into town to get dinner when Claire called and suggested they all meet at the hotel. Lucy thought it was a good idea, but for some reason, Marty hesitated.

"I think they've been really busy recently," he said.

Lucy shrugged. "It should be fine. It's a Sunday, so everyone's probably checked out for the week. Claire wouldn't suggest it if it were a problem."

"I still might sit this one out."

"Stop being a baby," Lucy said. "You're not going to avoid dinner with me when I risked getting pooped on for you. We're going."

Lucy went home to shower and change, and Marty offered to pick her up once she was ready.

As soon as they got to the hotel, it all became clear to Lucy. Marty initially suggested they go around the back "to avoid the crowds."

"What crowds?" Lucy asked as she marched toward the front door. "I like to do a once over at the bar, see if there are any eligible bachelors."

He followed her, at a distance, and while she was scoping out the bar patrons, Marty was waved over to the front desk. Lucy almost missed it, blustering around and leering at the bar patrons, but luckily she realized what was happening in time.

Lucy didn't recognize the woman behind the desk, but the woman clearly recognized Marty.

She decided to welcome herself into the conversation by walking over and announcing, "Hi, I'm Lucy."

"My cousin," Marty added.

"So nice to meet you! I'm Emma."

Emma. That was the name of Marty's troubles.

"Marty was just telling me about your hike. It sounded so nice."

Lucy nodded. "It was. Have you ever been?"

"No, unfortunately not yet." Emma let out a sigh. "Hopefully I'll get a chance to go soon, though."

Lucy was about to suggest that Marty could take her, but he was already changing the topic.

"We'd better get out of your way," he said, flashing a smile.

"Have fun!" Emma said, smiling brightly.

He walked away, and Lucy went after him.

"Marty," she whispered. "Was that the girl?"

He turned and glared at her. "*Sh!*"

"Oh, come on." Lucy trotted to catch up to him. "I told you about my boyfriend."

"Your ex-boyfriend," he corrected.

She couldn't help but laugh. He was so grumpy about this!

Claire and Chip were already waiting at the table, and Lucy decided to drop the subject for now.

Dinner was fantastic: Dungeness crab cakes and a tajarin ragu with braised beef. It was nice being back with family again. Living in the city got lonely. Though she was close, it still felt like she was so far away from everyone and everything exciting.

After dinner, they went back to Claire's house and sat around the fireplace chatting. Lucy waited to pounce until after Claire had excused herself to bed for the evening.

"I've been waiting all night to hear about Emma," Lucy said, "and I think you'll agree it was pretty good of me not to bring her up in front of Claire."

He offered a weak smile. "You could continue not to bring her up."

"Come on, Marty. She seemed like she liked you. What's the problem?"

"She's made it clear that she's not looking for a boyfriend."

"She said that to you?" Lucy crossed her arms. "Then forget her. She doesn't deserve you."

"She didn't say it to me exactly, but – "

"Hang on." Lucy put up a hand. "What did she say, then?"

"It's complicated."

"Tell me!" Lucy smiled. "I don't bite."

He let out a sigh and told her the brief history of Emma – everything from her liver transplant to her divorce to her crummy ex-husband and her missing cat.

"I'm trying to get the cat back, but I've been unsuccessful," Marty said. "I've messaged this woman three times and she won't respond to me."

Lucy clutched a hand to her chest. "Marty, this is so sweet."

"Don't start," he said, pointing a finger at her. "You've got to keep it together."

Lucy nodded. "You're right." She took a deep breath. "I wouldn't say that she doesn't like you. I know this is hard to hear, but you might actually have to talk to her."

"I was afraid you might say that."

"It's rough, but there's no getting around it."

Marty shifted in his seat. "I thought she wanted me to leave her alone, but then today she sent a text asking if she could take me to dinner."

"To dinner!" Lucy exclaimed.

"As a thank you," he continued. "For driving her to work for a week."

"That's still something." Lucy paused, thinking. "I mean, when I wanted to get away from my boss, I wouldn't have suggested hanging out with him. Also, if I knew a guy liked me and I didn't like him back, I wouldn't suggest hanging out with him..."

"She doesn't have any other friends around here." Marty shrugged. "She's just being nice."

"I don't know. I would say – "

He cut her off. "You're not the only one keeping secrets from Claire, you know."

Lucy's mouth popped open. "What!"

He pulled an envelope out of his pocket. "This was at my apartment today."

Lucy gasped, opening the letter. This one was handwritten.

Dear Marty,

I've been thinking about it and I think you'd be proud of me too. Not too proud, but I've done better for myself. I just wanted you to know that.

- B

She looked up at him. "What the heck is this? It sounds like it was written by a crazy person."

He laughed. "I don't know. These letters are making less and less sense."

"Did you dust it for fingerprints?"

Marty let out a groan and took the letter back. "How many times do I have to tell you it doesn't work that way?"

"Until you make it work that way," she said matter-of-factly. "What're you going to do?"

"I have no idea. This person has my address now. It's starting to get creepy."

"We should probably confront David and make sure it's not him," Lucy said.

"No," Marty said slowly. "I know David's handwriting, and it doesn't look like this."

"He could have gotten someone else to write it."

Marty shook his head. "I don't think so."

Lucy sat back on the couch. "I'm going to send him a nasty email, just to be sure."

"Please don't."

Lucy smiled. She wouldn't. For now. At least she'd gotten Marty to laugh.

But if they didn't figure out who was sending these weird letters soon, she might have to go after David after all.

Chapter Twenty

Still no word from Marty. Emma had texted him hours ago, asking him to dinner. At the end of her shift, she did her hand off to Addie and made her way to her car.

Maybe she was being too forward, asking him to dinner? It was a thank you, though. Nothing more.

Emma drove home, telling herself he might just be busy with his cousin. Lucy seemed so cool. Different from Marty, but in a way, Emma could see the resemblance. They were probably having a lot of fun and he wasn't looking at his phone.

When she got home, she decided that maybe Marty didn't want to go to dinner because he'd been forced to chauffeur her around by Margie and he was still annoyed by it. At the time, however, it didn't seem that way; he seemed cheerful about it, even bringing her coffee every morning.

Emma's phone went off and she leapt to grab it.

"That would be great. I'm free any night," Marty had written back.

What a relief. He must have been busy after all. She typed out a message, suggesting a restaurant in town on Thursday. He agreed, and she spent the next three days at work looking forward to seeing him again.

As she was getting ready that night, doing her hair and putting on makeup, Emma had to admit something to herself. The panic she felt when she thought Marty didn't want to see her meant something. Even if she didn't want it to mean something, it did.

She'd never had feelings for anyone other than Travis, so this whole ordeal was confusing for her. It seemed hard to deny now, though – the thought that he might not want to see her had sent her into a spiral.

What was she supposed to do with that? Emma had no idea.

She offered to pick Marty up, half-jokingly, but she was happy when he accepted. He looked as cute as ever when he emerged from his place. She'd planned to get out and knock on his door, but he had seen her coming and was already waiting.

They got to the restaurant and Emma felt like he was being quieter than usual. She asked how his visit went with Lucy, and he showed her some pictures from the hike they'd done at the falls.

"Oh my gosh, I would love to go there," Emma said with a sigh.

"I'd be happy to take you," Marty said.

Emma smiled at him. "I'd really like that. I hope you know..." Her voice trailed off.

"What?"

She cleared her throat and started again. "I hope you know that when I say I want to do something, I mean it. I'd like to go on all of these hikes with you. It's just been hard since I've been working so much."

For a moment, he looked surprised. He recovered quickly. "Of course. I understand. I'm sorry that you don't have much free time. How long are you planning to work both jobs?"

She bit her lip. "I haven't really planned that far ahead. I was hoping to build my savings back up."

He frowned. "You mean after Travis fleeced you?"

That was one way to put it. "He still won't let me see Dolto. I'm starting to get worried. What if something really did happen to him? What if he's sick?"

"You can't think like that. We'll find him."

She cocked her head to the side. "Find him? What do you mean?"

"Oh, I just mean you'll get him back. You have to."

She stared at him for a moment. Was he just being nice, or did he really believe that? Her dad said she was wasting her life crying over a cat.

Marty didn't seem to think that, though.

He reached into his pocket and pulled out an envelope. "I got another weird letter."

"No way!" She reached forward. "Can I read it?"

"Sure," he said.

She read it once, then again, confused even more the second time around. "Is this code for something?"

Marty shook his head. "I have no idea. It's just rambling."

"I know this place," Emma said, pointing to a logo on the top left corner of the page.

He leaned forward. "What place? It's a place?"

Emma nodded, pulling her phone out of her purse. "It is. I know that logo. It's for a cat café in Oregon. Eugene, I think. I follow them on Instagram."

"You're kidding." Marty leaned in to look at her phone. Their faces were so close...

"You're right, that's it!" he said, pointing. "Whoever wrote this letter must work at the cat rescue."

Emma winced. "I mean, they sell this stationary on their website. They also sell little hats, mugs – you know, for fundraising. All of the cats in the café are up for adoption."

"Have you ever bought anything from there?"

Emma shook her head. "No, but I donate sometimes."

"I have to go there," he said. "I'm going to call off work and drive down tomorrow."

Emma laughed. "Marty! That's crazy."

"These letters are crazy. I have to step up to their level."

She crossed her arms. "What if you find someone worse than David this time?"

He stared at her with a glint in his eye. "Are you worried about me?"

"Yes!" she said, her cheeks growing hot.

"Then you can come with me."

Emma laughed. "I don't have any time off for my job."

"Do you get sick days?"

She shook her head. "Nope, no sick days. I couldn't call off like that. It'd put them in a bind."

"Then I'll update you the whole way," he said. "How far is the drive?"

"I'm not sure."

They spent the rest of the evening planning the route, as well as looking up the staff at the cat café. Marty decided that all of them were potential suspects.

Emma didn't know what to think. She wanted him to find out who was sending the letters, but most of all, she wanted him to be safe.

She needed him to be safe. The thought of him disappearing from her life for any reason was too much to bear.

Chapter Twenty-one

Around four hours into his eight-hour trip, Marty started to wonder if it was a mistake to go alone.

Whom would he have brought, though? His first choice was Emma, but she had to work every day. Even if she had a day off, a long car trip wasn't how she should spend her time. She needed to get out and enjoy the magnificence of the island, not the Febrezed seats of Marty's old Kia.

Lucy probably would've tagged along, but she'd already gotten into trouble once because of him before. This was what he tried to gently explain to her when she called him at noon.

"Aren't you on your lunch break? Why does it sound like you're in a car?"

"Because I am in a car," Marty replied.

"Well, where are you going?" Lucy asked. "A midday hike? Can I come? I'm bored."

"Lucy, I don't know how to tell you this..."

"Ooh, wait," she cooed. "Is there someone else in the car with you?"

He let out a sigh. "No, I'm alone. I'm driving to Oregon."

Silence for a beat. "Oregon? For work?"

"No. It's because of the letter."

She gasped. "You used the fingerprints like I told you to!"

"No, but listen. Did you notice there was a logo in the upper left corner of that last letter? It looked like a cat and a ball of yarn?"

"Hm. Honestly, no. I didn't notice."

He continued. "Emma saw it, and she recognized it from a cat café in Eugene, Oregon. So that's where I'm headed. I'm going to find whoever sent this letter."

"How? If you don't have those fingerprints..."

Marty shook his head. Lucy watched too much TV. "I don't know. I'll figure it out when I get there."

"Why didn't you bring me?" Lucy asked.

It took her longer than he'd expected for her to come up with that complaint. "If I end up getting myself in trouble, I didn't want to drag you down with me again."

Lucy groaned. "Come on! You know I don't mind a little trouble."

"The last time you got involved in helping me, you ended up in FBI custody."

"Ah." She paused. "That's true, but not totally fair. That was David's fault. Everything is David's fault, now that I think about it."

"I'll be shocked if I find David in Eugene."

"I'll be shocked if you find *anyone* in Eugene. For all you know, David's mom could like the cat café stationary and he could've borrowed it."

Marty knew she was right, and yet... "I guess we'll see."

"You're crazy, Mr. Coursin," Lucy said. "I can't wait to hear more from you. Keep me updated, please!"

"I will."

He was already texting Emma every time he stopped. Not that he'd stopped much. The first time was when he got on the ferry, and the second was when he had to get gas. He'd even packed sandwiches so he could avoid scrounging for food along the way.

It paid off. Despite a bad crash near Portland, he made decent time and got to Eugene promptly at 3:15. It was a nice little town; what it lacked in high-rise buildings, it made up for with a huge, looming mountain in the distance.

However, Marty wasn't there to sightsee, so he went straight to the cat café. When he walked inside, he was somewhat disappointed that he didn't immediately recognize the person who'd been sending him the letters. No one looked familiar, and no one seemed surprised to see him.

"Hi!" said the woman from behind the counter. "What can I get you?"

It was only him and one other patron in the entire café, along with about ten cats. He ordered coffee and a scone, then debated asking questions of the woman behind the counter. Of all of the cat café employees, she seemed the least suspicious.

"Do you happen to recognize this handwriting?" he asked, producing the letter from his pocket.

The woman leaned in. "Can't say that I do. Sorry."

Marty thanked her and tucked it away. When he sat down with his coffee, he saw the logo everywhere – on notepads, scattered throughout the café, on the paper cups, even on the pens.

He could kick himself.

What if Lucy was right? He'd really jumped to some hefty conclusions by showing up here.

Still, he reasoned, there couldn't be that many regular patrons of this café. If he needed to sit here every day for two weeks, waiting for someone to come in and recognize him, he would do it. He could work remotely. Blaise didn't care, and Marty wasn't one to give up easily.

He sat in his seat until closing, working surprisingly efficiently on his laptop. He also efficiently burned through two coffees, a tea latte, an iced tea, another scone, and a ten-inch deli sandwich.

That was partially because everything looked so good, but also because he felt guilty for taking up a table all day.

Not that the place was busy, and that was a shame, really. They had wonderful cats. Marty donated a hundred dollars toward the adoption of a particularly friendly tabby who'd kept him company throughout the day. Despite the cramp in his neck, he decided this café was one of his top five favorite places to work.

Fifteen minutes before closing, he realized it was time to throw in the towel. He decided he'd come back again in the morning. On his way out, he asked the barista if she knew of any good hotels in the area.

"There are a bunch of hotels. They're all basically the same. Have you been to Eugene before?"

Marty shook his head. "This is my first time."

"Then you *have to* stay at one of the hostels. My favorite is probably the one at Paradise Skies."

Marty cocked his head to the side. "Paradise Skies?"

"It's one of the cohousing communities here. You can't get to know Eugene without knowing our communities."

Cohousing community. Was that a modern word for a commune? Oh man. "Aha, right. Cool."

"I have some friends there. You'll love it. There's complimentary goat's milk every morning."

Goat's milk. Exactly what he was hoping for. Marty reminded himself to smile. "Thank you. I'll check it out."

When he got back to his car, he'd planned to find the nearest Holiday Inn, but first had to text Emma about the experience. Unbelievably, she thought he should stay at the commune.

"When's the next time you'll get the chance to do that?" she argued.

He shut his eyes. This was *way* outside of his comfort zone. The sort of people who lived in a commune were probably also the sort of people who would want to chat with him.

Marty was terrible at talking to strangers. He liked living in the city for that reason. People mostly ignored him. He preferred to be ignored. On Orcas, people sometimes tried to get friendly, but he could usually get out of long conversations.

Marty let out a sigh. He wasn't going to look unadventurous to Emma. He typed the name of the commune into his phone and started the drive. It wasn't far from the cat café, and as he passed through the gates, he got the feeling he was in for an experience like no other.

There were fields and gardens on either side of the road with a river in the backdrop. He was navigating to the hostel, but it seemed that the little town didn't have roads for cars, so he had to park just outside of it.

He made the walk through what looked like the center of a small village. There were houses and little buildings lining the way, and even a general store with an old-timey sign.

If he was going to have to make small talk with strangers, he at least needed to get credit for this. He snapped a picture of the town and sent it to Emma. She wrote back immediately. "So cute!"

The hostel was tucked snugly into the village, and Marty found it easily. He took a deep breath before pulling the door open.

Inside there was a small lobby with no one behind the front desk. He didn't want to be a nuisance, but after five minutes of waiting, he rang the service bell.

A man emerged a few moments later. "Hey, friend. How are you today?"

His genuine smile creeped Marty out. "I'm good. How are you?"

"Good, always good! Are you looking for a place to lay your head tonight?"

Lay his head. Ugh. This was a mistake. "Um, yes."

"Then you've come to the right place." He flipped open a large book. "We've got single and double rooms, as well as our bunk room, which has three people in it right now. Tonight you're welcome to join us out by our fire pit. However, since it is a high burn risk time of year, we don't have a fire going, but we do have lights, conversation, and laughter."

"That sounds great," he lied. Marty couldn't think of the last time he'd felt so uncomfortable. It would only get worse if he went to the fire pit. He was fine with lights, but the conversation and laughter might send him over the edge.

He paid for a single room and was surprised at how clean and comfortable it was. He unpacked a few things, then sat on the small bed, debating what to do.

He texted both Emma and Lucy to see what they thought. Both gave him a resounding recommendation to go and meet people at the "light and laughter" event.

Marty had always been a loner. Being alone when he had to hide from the FBI hadn't been that tough on him. He didn't even mind living in the woods, dealing with the rain. He'd much rather deal with rain and mud than a group of friendly people.

Ugh, friendly people. An introvert's worst nightmare. Nothing about this communal gathering appealed to him. He knew the most likely outcome for the night would be him saying something stupid and embarrassing himself in front of these strangers. Then he would ruminate on how much of an idiot he was for weeks.

It was his pattern.

When he didn't respond to Emma's message, she messaged again, arguing the more people he met, the higher the chances were that he might meet someone who could help him.

Marty groaned when he read her message. He wasn't used to needing other's help. He could usually solve things on his own. If he couldn't, he'd just leave them broken. That was his usual solution.

It took him almost twenty minutes to psych himself up enough to step outside. As promised, there were people milling around, having drinks, talking and laughing.

It seemed like far too many people to be socializing for a weeknight. Didn't these people have jobs?

Maybe they didn't. Maybe that was the point. If they grew their own food and made their own clothing...

A woman caught Marty's eye, causing him to do a double take. It looked like Claire had just walked by him before disappearing behind a building.

His brain couldn't compute how that was possible. He went after her, catching up quickly, though he couldn't see her face. From behind, it clearly wasn't Claire. Her hair was long, almost down to her elbows, and it was streaked with gray.

This poor woman would think he was chasing her down. Marty stopped, feeling silly, when the woman suddenly turned around and locked eyes with him.

It wasn't Claire.

It was Becca.

Time froze. Marty could no longer hear the chatter, or the music, or even his own thoughts. He stared at the woman in front of him, and she stared back.

She broke the silence. "Howdy."

Marty took a step toward her. "Hi."

She smiled a partially toothless smile. "Can I help you with something?"

"Don't I know you?"

The smile was still frozen on her face. "People call me Mother around here."

Mother. That would make sense – for him. He cleared his throat. "Are you Rebecca Cooke?"

She took a deep breath and let out a laugh. "No one's called me Rebecca in a long time."

He stared at her, stunned.

She patted him on the shoulder and walked past. "Come on, you don't want to miss out on the festivities."

It took a moment for him to realize she was walking away. He went after her. "I'm Marty. Marty Coursin. I think I've been getting your letters."

"Oh yeah?"

He stopped. "Don't you recognize me?"

"'Course I do," she said, spinning around. "Welcome, Marty."

He narrowed his eyes. "I'm your – I think I'm your son."

"Of course you are!"

Marty stared at her, mouth open.

She put her hands out in an exaggerated shrug. "I'm sorry. I just didn't expect to see you here. It's like the FBI's Most Wanted List coming to life." She laughed. "Can I get you something to eat?"

Marty didn't know what else to say, so he said, "Okay."

He followed her back to the group near the fire pit and watched as she made her way to the grill, talking to a few others along the way.

Marty was too stunned to speak. After a few minutes, she returned and handed him a plate with a hot dog.

"This is vegan," she said. "Not sure if you're used to that sort of thing."

"Thanks," he said. He took a bite. It wasn't a hot dog, exactly, but it tasted fine.

She took a seat. "What brings you to Eugene?"

"I wanted to find out who was sending me those letters."

She nodded. "I should've known you'd find me. I didn't want you to."

"Why not?" he asked, taking a seat across from her.

She shrugged. "I didn't want to mess up your life. I didn't want to cause a problem."

He shook his head. "You're not causing a problem. Nobody knew that..." It was like his voice ran out. He had to clear his throat to get it going again. "No one knows you're alive. Not even Claire."

"You should keep it that way," she said, standing up and walking off again.

Marty followed her, leaving the dry hot dog lookalike behind. "Why? All these years, she thought she was alone, she thought – "

"But Claire isn't alone, is she?" Becca said, spinning around. "She has Lucy and Lillian and Rose. And you!"

"But – "

She cut him off. "You know who's alone? Me."

Marty shook his head. "You don't have to be alone."

"I'm not!" she said, waving a hand behind her. "These people are my family. I'm a member of the community. I keep a job, I garden, I volunteer at the café. I've turned my life around. It took years, and I mean *years*, but I turned it around."

"If they knew that..."

"They're not going to find out," Becca said firmly. "I won't have you messing my life up either. Do you understand?"

None of this made any sense. His mind was spinning. She seemed so *angry.*

Becca let out a heavy sigh. "Why don't you enjoy the get-together? In the morning, I can show you around if you'd like."

Marty nodded. She walked off, joining a conversation with a small group of people standing in a circle.

Marty hung out in her periphery, waiting, for half an hour. At one point, she joined in a song.

He couldn't take any more of this. If she came looking for him in the morning, he wouldn't be there.

Chapter Twenty-two

It was too quiet on Orcas Island for Lucy's tastes. Claire was busy, and she hadn't heard back from Marty about what he'd decided to do at the commune. He'd probably ignored her advice and gone straight to bed. That seemed like the Marty thing to do.

Frustratingly, the next morning he didn't answer her messages. Lucy started to wonder if he really did find someone.

But no. That was impossible. He was on a wild goose chase, and he was probably just starting to get annoyed that nothing was working out. She decided not to poke the wound by asking about it.

Instead, she went to Eastsound to embrace the day. She got breakfast at a bakery in town, then walked around looking at the shops. Eventually she wandered into the Orcas Island Historical Museum and got into a lively conversation with a volunteer about a historical map on display.

The island wasn't that big, but Lucy felt like she learned something new about it every time she visited. The museum was the newest addition to that. She walked through, engrossed by the old pictures of settlers on the island.

It was cute and all, but Lucy was thankful to be alive in current times. Even just a hundred years ago, life on the island would have been too rugged for her tastes.

She was headed back to the bakery to get another cup of coffee when she saw a flyer about a yoga class in town. It was supposed to start in an hour. Lucy rushed back to Claire's house, changed, and jumped headfirst into the class.

The instructor wasn't her favorite, but she enjoyed it enough. Once it was done, she couldn't come up with anything else to do. Her only choice was to go back to the house and face what she'd been avoiding: finding a new job.

It was a Herculean task. Applying was easy enough. Even getting interviews wasn't that hard. She'd had so much experience that she could fill a number of different roles.

The problem was something else – it was a problem with Lucy. She never ended up liking any of these jobs. She'd start out sunny and optimistic, then grow restless, and inevitably quit. It was a pattern, and she knew it, but she didn't know how to break it.

Nevertheless, she dutifully applied to a handful of jobs before shutting off her computer and declaring she'd done more than enough for one day.

If only Claire weren't so busy with the hotel. Lucy was glad Claire had the hotel, because she seemed so blissfully happy, but it also made her wonder. Had Claire known she would love owning a hotel? How come Lucy didn't know anything about herself?

She took a shower and decided to pop into the local library, using Claire's library card to pick out some books. It worked, and she went home and read a delightful book by Matt Haig for a few hours.

After her neck started to get stiff, she decided to head over to the hotel and see what Claire and Chip were up to.

To her surprise and delight, Emma was working reception. Lucy immediately went over to chat with her.

"Hey!" she said brightly.

Emma smiled. "Hi Lucy! How's it going?"

"Pretty good," she said. "I didn't know you worked here during the week."

"Usually I don't," Emma said, shaking her head. "But Gigi had an emergency and had to leave halfway through her shift, so Claire called and asked if I could come and fill in after I finished up at the daycare."

"You work at a daycare? Why didn't I know that?"

Emma smiled. "I guess we didn't have much time to talk before."

Lucy nodded. "Very true. Have you heard from Marty today? I think he's ignoring me."

"He hasn't been answering me, either," she said, dropping her voice. "He told me that he's on his way back. Do you think something happened to him?"

Lucy waved a hand. "No way. You know he lived in the woods by himself for a few weeks, right?"

"This is different," Emma said. She looked totally unconvinced. "I don't know why he insists on showing up and looking for people."

"The boldness of youth, I guess," Lucy said with a laugh.

She didn't know why she said that. Marty wasn't a particularly bold person, just impulsive. He also wasn't all that youthful.

A couple got in line behind Lucy and she moved out of the way so Emma could help them. Once they were gone, Lucy stepped back up. "How's it going? Is it busy tonight?"

"Oh, a bit. I like being busy."

"Do you like working here?" asked Lucy.

"Very much!"

Lucy let out a sigh. "You don't have to lie to me because my mom owns the place. I won't tell."

Emma smiled and shook her head. "No, really, I like it."

She seemed to mean it. Odd. Lucy leaned in, resting her chin on her hand. "What do you like about it? And what do you like about working at the daycare?"

"I love kids," Emma said. "They're so cute and fun and – "

Lucy groaned. "That's enough. I can't relate to that. I never really got along with kids."

"Why do you ask?"

"I'm looking for a new career," Lucy said. "Trying to figure out what makes other people happy in their jobs. I know I'm old to still be looking, but nothing ever seems to fit."

Emma frowned. "I'm sorry to hear that."

"Did you always want to work with kids?"

"Yeah, always," Emma said with a smile. "I wanted to be a teacher. Hopefully I will be someday."

"You're too much," Lucy said, shaking her head. "You're too genuinely sweet. I can't take advice from you."

They laughed, and three more people got in line behind Lucy. She stepped out of the way and watched Emma work. She was pleasant to all of them, even though the last guy was quite rude and talked on his phone throughout their entire interaction, treating Emma like she was interrupting him by doing her job.

Lucy had always had problems with customer-facing jobs. When someone was rude to her, her instinct was to be rude back. That was a no-no, though, and got her several work demerits. The demerits also made her laugh, because it was like she was getting detention.

Lucy thought Emma would finally have a break and be able to talk again when yet another couple stepped up behind her. She had half a mind to tell them to buzz off, but the look on Emma's face caught her attention.

"I didn't know you worked here," the woman said.

Emma nodded, a stiff smile on her face. "Yeah, just here and there. Do you have a reservation?"

"Yes. Under Travis Dickinson," the guy said.

Travis. Travis. Why did that name ring a bell? Lucy couldn't place it.

"Okay, we've got you in a queen on the first floor."

"Can't you give us an upgrade?" Travis asked.

Lucy angled herself to look at him. He had a stupid haircut and an annoyingly goofy-looking smile. Was it goofy, or was it smug?

"I apologize. We're totally booked this weekend," Emma said.

"Leave her alone," said the woman. "I'm sure it'll be a nice room. We just wanted a little weekend getaway. This will be perfect."

Emma worked quickly, passing the keys across the counter a moment later. "How's Dolto? You could've brought him," she said with a little laugh.

Travis snatched the keys and picked up his bag. "Uh, no, I don't think so."

Why did this smug man start to stammer all of a sudden? And why wasn't he helping his wife with her stuff? Her bag looked enormous and heavy, but still. He should try to be a gentleman.

Travis' companion cut him off. "I'm sorry. Didn't Travis tell you?" She turned to Travis. "You told me you told her."

"Told me what?" Emma asked, her voice small.

Lucy was clutching the pillar next to her so tightly that she was losing circulation in her hand. It all hit her at once.

Travis was Emma's ex-husband. Dolto was the cat! The woman must be...Kimmy, was it?

Lucy didn't want to be here. She didn't want to witness this drama. Why wasn't someone making it stop!

"Told me what?" Emma asked again.

Kimmy shot Travis a disgusted look. "I'm sorry, Emma, but Travis gave Dolto away. I thought you knew."

"Gave Dolto away?" The color drained from Emma's face. "Why? Why would you do that?"

Kimmy resisted Travis' tug on her arm. "I'm sorry, I thought your friend Marty would've told you."

"Marty?" Emma shook her head. "What does Marty have to do with it?"

Oh dear. Oh no. This was going from bad to worse.

Travis grabbed Kimmy firmly by the arm. "Let's go. We already got in late because of that stupid ferry and I don't want to pay for a room that we don't get to see."

They walked away, and Lucy took a cautious look at Emma. It looked like a stiff breeze could blow her over. Her big, brown eyes were searching everywhere, darting back and forth.

"Are you okay?" asked Lucy.

Emma nodded hurriedly, forcing a smile. "Yes, I'm fine. Everything's fine."

Lucy's stomach sank. Things were clearly not fine, and she felt powerless to fix them. She never should've left the house. She should've stayed home, applying to jobs like a normal person.

Heck, she could've even read her book! In books, bad things happened to *other* people. Fictional people. Not the people standing right in front of her, with a history of a nasty divorce and a severe illness. Not people with real, actual tears in their eyes.

Lucy cleared her throat. “Hey, how about I take over? I’m sure Claire wouldn’t mind.”

Emma pursed her lips together and shook her head. “I should get back to work. Have a nice evening, Lucy.”

Yikes. Lucy forced a smile and took the hint, walking out of the hotel and calling the only person who stood a chance of fixing this: Marty.

Chapter Twenty-three

The rest of her shift was a struggle. Emma tried to be professional. She didn't think the guests noticed, and she didn't want to be dramatic, but it felt like she was slowly dying.

Her chest was heavy, making it hard to take deep breaths. Her head pounded, and if she thought about Dolto or Marty, tears clouded her vision.

It was a relief when Addie arrived to take over.

"Are you okay? You don't look so good," Addie said, putting a hand to Emma's forehead.

Emma nodded. "I'm just tired."

That was true, at least. It was the end of a long week and somehow she needed to come back at the hotel in a few hours for her next shift.

What was it all for, though? Travis had given Dolto away. He had *given* him to a stranger, to someone who didn't even love him. She'd been such a fool, waiting and hoping and wishing she'd get him back. Why hadn't she done more? Why did she ever believe in Travis?

Or in Marty. He knew Travis had given Dolto away, and he hadn't done anything? He didn't even tell her?

What kind of a person – no, what kind of a friend – would do that? Emma had thought they were friends. Marty acted like he was so different from Travis – more understanding, more caring, more gentle.

It was all a lie. Marty wasn't some great guy. He was just another Travis. Maybe all guys were Travises. Even her dad was a Travis. He was the original one, at least.

Emma saw it all so clearly now. She'd gone from growing up with a dad who constantly criticized her and put her down to having a husband who did the same thing.

Was that all she could attract? Why had it taken her so long to notice?

When Marty called her that night, leaving her a frantic voicemail, she ignored it. Lucy must've told him what had happened.

Unfortunately, she couldn't avoid him. He found her at the hotel the next morning, and she was even more tired after a night of crying.

"Emma, I can explain," he said.

She told Gigi she was taking her break and pulled Marty aside. "I don't want to hear it, Marty."

"Kimmy told me that they gave Dolto away, but I've been trying to get him back."

"Without telling me? Why would you hide that from me?"

He grimaced. "I didn't want to worry you, and I wasn't sure if Kimmy was telling the truth. I thought I would have him back in no time."

"He's *my* cat, Marty. I'm the one that raised him from two weeks old, bottle feeding him every two hours, staying up with him all night." Emma couldn't keep the edge out of her voice. Not that she was trying terribly hard. "I'm the one that thinks about him every day."

He stared at her, eyes wide.

She couldn't stop. "Yet you're the one who decided I didn't deserve to know what happened to him? That I didn't deserve a chance to get him back myself?"

"Obviously I made the wrong choice," Marty said. "I am so, so, sorry, but if you'd let me make it up to you – "

"No." She could barely control her breathing, heavy and ragged. She hadn't felt this angry in...well, perhaps ever. "I don't want your help. If you want to do me a favor, leave me alone."

She turned on her heel and left him standing there, his mouth hanging open.

Mercifully, he didn't come after her. He disappeared, and Emma was left to finish her shift in peace.

Chapter Twenty-four

The moment Marty walked in the door, Lucy asked, "Was Emma there? How did it go?"

Marty flopped onto the couch and put his head in his hands. "She doesn't want me to speak to her again, so that's nice."

"Oh boy." Lucy took a seat next to him.

Marty still hadn't told her about his trip to Oregon. He didn't know what to say; it seemed best not to think about it.

Lucy had initially called him on his drive back up. He'd considered telling her what had happened then, but she'd immediately launched into a story about Travis and Emma at the hotel.

That was somehow worse than meeting his secretly-alive mom who wanted nothing to do with him.

No wonder his parents had never told him about Becca. When he first found out he'd been adopted, he was so hurt and betrayed. It felt like his parents had been lying to him, maliciously, for years.

Yet after many long conversations with both his mom and his dad, he'd realized it was never their intention to hurt him, or to hide anything from him. They were flawed, but not as flawed as Becca. She'd dismissed him so easily. He'd never felt so small in his life. His parents, despite their missteps, had done everything out of love, even if it was sometimes misguided.

Kind of like his stupid idea to not tell Emma that Dolto had been given away.

He looked up and realized Lucy was staring at him.

"Do you want something to eat?" she asked.

"No thanks."

She let out a sigh. "Just give Emma some time. She'll come around."

She was right. Marty shook his head. "I was an idiot not to tell her about Dolto. I think I can do everything on my own, and clearly I can't."

"That's not true. You're really good at things." Lucy paused. "But sometimes you might need to admit to yourself that teamwork makes the dream work."

Marty turned to face her. "That's one of the lamest things I've ever heard."

"I know," Lucy said with a laugh. "They used to say that at my old job."

"That's awful."

She laughed again. "I wanted to lighten the mood! Anyway, when I figured out they weren't joking, that's when I knew I had to quit."

"I thought it was because you broke up with your boss?"

"The combination, really. It was too much to bear."

Marty smiled. How did Lucy always find the bright side of things? He needed to be more like her.

Right now, though, he felt hopeless. He was a jerk. Emma was right. She was right to be angry at him. She was right to never want to see him again. He'd never be able to make it up to her.

Unless...

Marty got up. "Can I borrow your laptop?"

"Why?"

"I'm going to go and get Dolto."

Lucy frowned, but did as he asked and fetched her laptop from the other room. "How are you going to do that?"

"I'm going to show up at this lady's house with a bunch of money and beg."

"Marty," Lucy said slowly, "why is your first instinct always to go and surprise people?"

He stared her for a beat. "Because it works?"

"Fine." She shrugged. "But I'm coming with you."

"What?" He shook his head. "No."

"So you'll go by yourself? How did that go last time? You didn't find anything, did you? Because you're antisocial."

He stopped what he was doing to look at her. "I did find something."

She crossed her arms. "Oh yeah? What?"

This might not be the best time to tell her, but there was no time like the present. "I found the person who sent the letters."

Lucy let out a little gasp. "Who was it? How did you find them?"

"Dumb luck, honestly." He let out a sigh. "The person sending the letters was Becca."

Lucy's expression didn't change for a moment. It was like she was frozen. Finally she said, "I'm sorry, I think I just hallucinated. Who did you say sent those letters?"

Yeah, this wasn't the right time. It was too late now, though. "She's alive, Lucy."

Lucy nodded, then held up a finger telling him to wait. "I think I'm going to throw up."

"I'm sorry. I didn't know how to tell you."

Lucy wagged her finger at him and he fell silent. She stood, went to the kitchen, and poured herself a glass of water. After drinking the entire thing, she returned to the couch. "Okay, so you went out to the desert and saw a mirage of your dead biological mother."

"Eugene isn't in the desert."

She rolled her eyes. "Marty! Not the point!"

He continued. "I went to a commune and saw my biological mother."

"Have you told Claire yet?"

"I haven't told anyone except for you." Marty shook his head. "You're my test, and you're not taking the news well."

Lucy's mouth hung open. "You didn't really prepare me for it!"

"She told me not to tell anyone she's alive."

"What?" Lucy narrowed her eyes. "Why?"

"Who knows," Marty said with a shrug. "She said she's not going to let me mess up the life she's made or something. Whatever. I don't need her."

"Marty, this is unreal. We have to tell Claire."

He nodded. "I don't know how. I'm obviously not going to hide it from her. I've learned my lesson on hiding things."

Lucy put a hand over her mouth. "This feels like an out of body experience. Claire always used to say she had a feeling about Becca. How crazy is that? She was right!"

"I don't know what I was expecting. I mean, I didn't really think she was the one sending the letters, but when I met her, she was so flippant. She seemed surprised I'd found her, but not excited to meet me or anything."

"I'm so sorry, Marty."

He straightened his back. "Don't be. I don't need her. I have parents, and I have you guys." He paused. He'd had a lot of time to think on his drive back. "You know, when you're adopted, you think meeting your birth parents is going to mean something, or tell you something about yourself. But all I need is my mom, my dad, you, Claire, Lillian and Rose. That tells me enough. I don't need someone who doesn't want me."

Lucy made a face, pinching her lips together. "You're going to make me cry."

"Try not to, Lucy," he said, turning back to the screen. "I've got the lady's address. Are you in?"

Lucy took a deep breath. "I guess I asked for this. Are we going to go right now?"

"Right now," he said with a nod.

"All right, I'm in."

They got into Marty's car, drove two miles down the road, and blew a tire.

"Okay," Marty said, surveying the damage. "Maybe not right now. But very soon."

Lucy nodded. "Got it. Can we take my car?"

"No. I'll get this fixed. Just hang on."

Chapter Twenty-five

It was difficult for Emma to get through her shift on Saturday, and even more difficult to come back Sunday morning. She was exhausted, physically and emotionally.

Still, she couldn't stop thinking about Marty. It seemed like he'd fallen off the face of the earth. She'd wanted him to leave her alone, yet somehow, she didn't expect him to take it so literally.

What did that make her? Emma had no idea. The whole ordeal tormented her, ripping through her thoughts and keeping her awake at night. Against her instincts, she got close to trusting Marty, and then...

Poof. All lies.

Deep down, she knew she would never get Dolto back. It was a hope she'd clung to, simply because the truth was too hard to face. People went their whole lives believing comforting lies. Why did hers always have to come crashing down?

Her greatest wish was that Dolto would be healthy, happy, and safe. If only she could know he was safe and loved, she would have some peace.

Yet even when Marty had known where Dolto was, he'd kept it from her. Why would he hide it? Did he know Dolto was in trouble?

Emma knew it was her fault that she hadn't fought to keep him safe. All those years ago, she'd promised to take care of him. To love him. To protect him, always. She said it with every kiss, and he thanked her with ever purr, every snuggle, every time he rushed to the door to greet her when she got home.

As angry as she was with Marty, it was her fault that Dolto was gone. She had to live with that.

Around ten on Sunday, Claire stopped by the reception desk.

"Just checking in to see how you're doing," she said.

Emma took a deep breath and forced a smile. "I'm good. How are you?"

"I don't mean this in a rude way," Claire said slowly, "but you don't seem like yourself. I'm afraid we might have overworked you by asking you to come in and cover for Gigi."

"No, it was fine," Emma said, making her voice as light as she could. She felt a bit dizzy, but that was because she hadn't slept, and she was dehydrated from crying so much. And she hadn't eaten. Also, because of her poor judgment, she didn't have a single friend on the island and had made a huge mistake moving here.

"No." Claire let out a tsk. "I overdid it. I want you to go home for the rest of the day and relax."

"It's really okay."

"Come on, move over," Claire said, gently pushing Emma aside. "I will man the desk until Addie gets here. You go home and relax. Consider this a paid break. You more than deserve it."

Emma stared at her. She knew she should protest, but she felt like she would burst into tears. Somehow it was always harder to keep her composure when someone was kind to her than when they were cruel. "Thank you, Claire. This is really nice."

Claire reached out and squeezed Emma's shoulder. "You're welcome."

When Emma got to her car, her feelings swelled to the surface. Though she was grateful to Claire, she also felt guilty. Did Lucy put her up to it, or did Claire think she was slacking on the job?

Emma couldn't bear it if that were the case. Between the hours she'd been working, her fight with Marty, losing Dolto, and not sleeping, it seemed like any little thing could push her over the edge.

Emma wasn't normally like this. She was ashamed of herself for being such a mess. People had much more difficult lives than she did. She knew that. She felt it in her soul.

Yet, at this moment, she couldn't escape her own feelings. All she could do was force herself to drive.

Emma's first idea was to go home and take a nap, but when she drove through town, a restaurant caught her eye. It was a Mexican place she'd longed to try. It looked like they were just opening, and they had a sign out for a lunch special.

There was even a parking spot right next to the building. Her car glided into it. She told herself she needed a distraction to keep herself from slipping into an overtired, hysteric mess.

It wasn't difficult to enjoy herself. The staff was exceedingly kind, starting her meal with a complementary order of chips, guacamole, and queso. That alone was enough to fill her stomach, yet she still ate two of her three fish tacos.

The waitress offered her a free dessert as well: sopapillas, which looked like puffy fried dough with powdered sugar. Emma had to decline, for fear that she might explode, but she thanked the waitress profusely.

She had no idea what she did to deserve such kindness, first from Claire and now at the restaurant, but she decided to pass it forward somehow.

After lunch, she went home and took a short, coma-like nap. The food put her right out, or perhaps it was the fact that her mind wasn't racing for the first time in days.

Either way, the nap set her straight. When she woke up, she felt better. Her feelings weren't overwhelming her, and she decided to use the day as best she could.

Emma got into her car and set her navigation to Mt. Constitution.

The drive was surprisingly long and steep, winding through the forest. Emma drove slowly, admiring the beauty and feeling slightly afraid that her car might break down and block the narrow road.

Her fears didn't come true, and she reached the parking lot near the top of the mountain. She parked and took the hilly walkway to the lookout area.

Finally, she had some views. Emma stood back at first, afraid of getting too close to the edge. Despite the stone fence, she was still frightened about being so high. Fortunately, even from the safety of fifteen feet away, the view was spectacular. She could see miles into the distance.

There were picnic tables midway to the wall, and Emma decided that was a good spot to start. She took a seat and felt like she was on stable ground for the first time.

Beneath her, she could see thousands of pine trees that looked too green and uniform and perfect to be true. The end of the island met the ocean, which twinkled in the sun, spanning into the horizon. There were islands in the distance, and mountains too.

She wasn't sure what she was looking at, so once she felt like she wouldn't blow away, she checked an informational sign pointing out what everything was. From her view, she was seeing Blakely Island, Lummi Island, Bellingham in the distance, and the faint outline of Mt. Baker beyond that.

Amazing. She smiled and took a cautious step closer to the wall. The other people walking around didn't seem as afraid as she was. It wasn't dangerous at all. It just felt that way.

Emma managed to snap a few pictures with her phone. She wanted to send one to her mom, but she had no service. It would have to wait.

Her final stop, she decided, would be the viewing tower. Built from handsome gray stone and seemingly impermeable to the wind, Emma felt secure as she climbed the stairs. On each floor, there were placards describing how the tower was built by the CCC in the 1930s. In the 1940s, they added antenna to it for radio and television. It looked much better now without the attachments, she thought.

When Emma got to the top, the views were even more breathtaking. There were more signs, too, pointing out the Cascade Mountains and Anacortes in the distance. She was so involved in looking at them that she didn't realize someone else had climbed the tower. Emma was poring over the signs when she walked directly into the woman.

"I'm so sorry," Emma said.

The woman waved a hand. "Don't worry about it."

Emma saw her face and gasped.

"Are you all right?" the woman asked.

"You look..." Emma's voice trailed off.

The woman narrowed her eyes. "I can't hear you over this wind."

Emma raised her voice. "You look so much like someone I know."

"Oh yeah?" The woman turned to look out over the water. "Who's that?"

Emma cleared her throat. Perhaps she wasn't as well rested as she thought. Perhaps she was seeing things. "My boss, Claire Cooke."

The woman grunted. "She a good boss?"

Emma took a step closer. Yes, this woman absolutely looked like Claire, perhaps ten years in the future. Her skin was more wrinkled and tanned by the sun. The eyes, though. They were the same. "She is. She made me leave early today because she thought I was overworked."

"How about that." The woman let out a chuckle and tried to light a cigarette, shielding it from the wind. "You don't mind, do you?"

Emma shook her head. "Do you know Claire?"

She nodded. "I did once."

"I'm sorry, but are you related?"

She took a long drag of the cigarette, which had finally come to life. "You could say that. She's my sister."

This wasn't happening. Emma stumbled back slightly into the stone wall.

"Do me a favor?" the woman asked.

Emma nodded.

"Don't tell her you saw me, all right?"

The woman turned to leave and Emma reached to grab her elbow. "Wait!"

She stopped.

"Are you Becca?"

She stared back with those green eyes. Claire's eyes. Marty's eyes. "I am."

"Why don't you want her to know you're here?"

Becca scratched her head. "This isn't the first time I've come here. To the island. I drove to Seattle a couple times, too. I could never do it."

"Do what?"

"Come back from the dead!" Becca said with a roaring laugh.

Emma flashed a smile, more because she felt awkward than anything. "I can only imagine how much she wants to see you."

Becca shrugged, tamping out her cigarette on the stone. The wind had already defeated it. "After all those years I wasted? Letting her think I was dead? She won't thank me for it."

"What about all the years that you'll waste if you don't tell her?" Emma said quietly.

Becca said nothing, turning to leave again.

"What about Marty?" Emma knew she'd heard her that time. She'd said his name quite loud.

Becca turned, locking her eyes onto Emma's. "What do you know about Marty?"

"We're friends. He's...." Her voice trailed off.

What was the truth about Marty? She didn't truly believe he was a bad guy. She knew he was a decent person. Perhaps he tried too hard to be good, too hard to be noble. It was his dumb nobleness that landed him on the run from the FBI.

Emma knew that in her heart, she'd already forgiven him. He wasn't a Travis. It was unfair to label him as such.

"He's a wonderful person," she said.

Becca looked out over the water again. "He came to see me, and then he just disappeared."

Emma cocked her head to the side. "What? When?"

"The other day. Showed up out of the blue. Scared the pants off of me. I didn't welcome him like I should've." Becca shook her head. "I knew I would never be a good mother, and even just meeting him, I managed to be a disappointment." Becca puffed out her cheeks, sniffled, then turned toward the stairs. "They're better off without me."

"No, they're not." Emma crossed her arms. "You're just afraid."

Becca smirked. "Nah."

"You're frightened." Emma smiled. She knew a thing or two about fear. "You're making excuses. If you give up that easily on getting to know Marty, though, then you're right. You don't deserve to know him."

Becca cracked a smile. "You don't pull your punches, do you, girl?"

"I'm learning," Emma said, suddenly worried she'd said too much. She looked down at her shoes.

"What's your name?"

"Emma."

Becca patted her on the shoulder. "Thanks for the pep talk, Emma."

With that, Becca left. Emma stayed at the top of the tower, watching as she walked toward the parking lot, disappearing amongst the trees.

Emma no longer felt the cold from the wind. She no longer felt guilty about having time off that day, either, or about people being nice to her.

The day had gone exactly as it was supposed to. She felt a warmth in her chest. Whatever mess of emotions brought her to the top of that mountain had been the right mix after all.

Chapter Twenty-six

With a new tire, Marty and Lucy hit the road. Lucy started questioning him immediately, forcing Marty to admit he didn't have much of a plan.

"Showing up with a wad of cash isn't as effective as you might think it is," Lucy argued.

Marty disagreed with her. "It would've worked on Kimmy. If I'd talked to her, like, a week sooner, Dolto would've been mine."

"This woman isn't Kimmy," Lucy countered.

"True, this is Juno. Juno..."

"Juno Marsh," Lucy said sternly. "Learn her name! My gosh, Marty!"

"Right." He kept his eyes on the road. "I've increased my bounty. It's going to work."

Lucy scoffed. "Is it," she said flatly.

He pressed her for details about what she thought would work, but she didn't have any more of a plan than he did. She insisted she'd feel it out when they got there.

"Is that what you did right before David turned you into the FBI?" Marty asked with a smirk.

"That was a peculiar situation," Lucy said, arms crossed. "How was I supposed to know David had such poor judgment?"

That made Marty laugh. "Except for the fact I told you not to talk to him?"

"You didn't tell me *why*," Lucy said. "See, in the end, it's your fault. You can be a poor communicator, you know."

He shrugged. "I agree with you there."

They bickered for much of the trip. Even so, Marty thought it was far more pleasant to drive with someone than to drive alone, like he had to Oregon.

He was certain a plan would come to him sometime during the four-hour trip, but nothing materialized. When they pulled in front of Juno's house, he didn't even have an opening line. How would he introduce himself without sounding like a creep?

"Maybe I should do the talking?" Lucy suggested.

He made a face. "No, that makes me nervous. Just follow my lead, okay?"

She rolled her eyes but didn't protest.

They walked up to the front door and Marty rang the doorbell. They stood there, listening to the sound of children playing down the street.

Marty could still hear his heartbeat in his ears. This was his last chance to get Dolto. He knew that. He couldn't mess it up.

A child around ten years old opened the door and smiled.

Marty was not expecting this. "Hi. Is your mom home?"

The kid shook his head. "No."

Lucy shot a look at Marty, then turned to the boy. "How about your grandma? Or a babysitter?"

He seemed to consider this for a moment, then turned and walked away.

"Should we follow him in?" asked Marty in a low voice.

"No!" Lucy replied, her voice hushed. "We need to wait here until he comes back with someone. We can't go barging into the house."

Lucy was right. Marty's desperation was making it hard to think.

An older woman came to the door, and Marty recognized her from the pictures. It was Juno.

She looked at the two of them and frowned. "I'm not interested in whatever you're selling, but thank you."

"We're not selling anything," Marty said quickly. "I was actually hoping to buy something from you."

She chuckled. "I don't like the sound of that either."

"My name is Marty," he continued. "I tried to contact you on Facebook about your new cat, Dolto? You got him from a guy named Travis?"

Juno crossed her arms. "I don't know what you're talking about."

Marty frowned. Maybe he had the wrong house? It was possible. He was working off online records, they could have been wrong. Or Kimmy might have lied.

After an awkwardly long pause, Lucy spoke up. "I'm sorry. Mrs. Marsh?"

She let out a sigh. "Yes?"

"My cousin Marty doesn't have the best people skills. I'm sorry about him. I'm Lucy." Lucy stuck out her hand.

Juno shook it. "Hi, Lucy."

"This is going to sound like a crazy story, and that's because it is. We're trying to get Dolto back for our friend Emma. She was married to Travis, but when she got sick and had to have a liver transplant, he divorced her. In the divorce, he kept her cat. We're just trying to reunite them."

Juno looked over her shoulder, then back at Lucy. "Is that so?"

"Yes!" She nodded eagerly. "I can show you pictures of Emma and Dolto."

"Why isn't Emma here?"

"Oh, that's simple." Lucy beamed. "My cousin's a bit of an idiot. He thought it would be romantic if he could get Dolto back for her as a surprise. I'm pretty sure he's in love with her. With Emma, that is. Not the cat."

Marty shut his eyes. This was a disaster.

Miraculously, a moment later, Juno let out a hearty laugh. "Would you two like to come inside?"

"That would be lovely," Lucy said.

A jolt ran through Marty's heart. She'd done it! She'd really done it! How had Lucy managed it? He had no idea. Marty kept his mouth shut and silently followed Lucy inside.

"Careful not to let the cats out," Juno said. "Last time Oreo snuck out, it took me two weeks to figure out she was hiding under the porch, crying."

Marty made sure the door was firmly latched behind him. Juno motioned for them to sit on the couch, and the young kid returned, bouncing at Juno's side.

"Do you want to see me play the drums?" he asked.

Juno patted him on the shoulder. "Not right now, sweetie. We need to talk about other things."

He shrugged and ran up the stairs.

"Is that your grandson?" Lucy asked.

Juno nodded. "Yes, that's William. He stays with me when his mom is at work."

Lucy nodded. "He's a cutie."

"Why, thank you. I think so too. He loves the cats, but I'm afraid he's a little allergic."

"How many cats do you have?" Lucy asked.

"Four," Juno said, shaking her head. "It's becoming a bit of a group. There are just so many cats who need a good home. I wish I could have a dozen more."

Marty felt the urge to say something, but he didn't know what. He wasn't good at jumping into conversations, and Lucy seemed to be doing so well on her own.

"Is that why you got Dolto?"

Juno rapped her fingers on the back of her hand, a pensive look on her face. "I saw that he was being given away on Facebook. Actually, a friend of mine sent the post to me. He's a beautiful cat, but the poster – Travis, was it?"

Marty nodded.

"Travis said if no one wanted him by the end of the day, he'd drop him at the shelter. It was urgent."

Marty could feel his temper flaring. "Unbelievable."

"Yeah, that sounds just like him." Lucy pulled her phone out of her pocket. "Do you want to see some pictures of Emma and Dolto?"

"I suppose so."

Lucy got up and sat next to Juno, flipping through pictures on her phone.

Marty was in awe. Where had she gotten those? They were on Facebook, so maybe she'd saved them?

Brilliant. Brilliant all around.

"He looked so happy," Juno said.

"He was happy. Oh, hang on, I have some from when he was little." Lucy clicked around for a moment. "Emma raised him from when he was only a few weeks old. Bottle fed him and everything."

"Look at his little face! He was so sweet." Juno looked up from the phone and shook her head. "I'm sorry about not letting you in earlier. I knew there was something funny going on with Dolto. My goal was to keep him safe."

"Emma has barely gotten to see him since the divorce," Lucy said. "If you're willing, I'm sure we can get her here to visit. I think when you see how Dolto reacts to her, you'll know she's his real owner."

Juno smiled. "Are you folks from around here?"

"A few hours away," Lucy said. "On Orcas Island."

She put her hand to her chest. "Now that's a trip!"

"We don't mind," Marty said. "I know Emma would do anything to get Dolto back."

"To tell you the truth, he's had a hard time adjusting here," Juno said, slowly rising from the couch. "I feel bad for the poor guy. The first week, he wouldn't eat. I was worried about him and was looking for a new home for him."

Marty perked up. "Please, Emma loves him more than anything. I'm sure we can get her here."

Juno smiled warmly and held up a hand. "Far be it from me to keep him away from his person."

Marty cleared his throat. "I also have two thousand – "

Lucy subtly kicked him before cutting him off. "I know it's strange for us to drop in like this, but this has been a long, ongoing saga."

"I didn't like that Travis at all when I met him," Juno said. "I could tell he had a nasty temper, you know? Even in the way he gave me Dolto. He just shoved the carrier in my hands, really rough."

"I can't stand him," Marty said.

Juno laughed. "You and me both. Well, if you want to follow me, I'll show you where Dolto's been staying."

They stepped over a few toys and Marty noticed two curious cats had started following them. Juno opened the door to a small laundry room and they stepped inside.

She flicked on the light. "He's been staying here, keeping mostly to himself. He started to eat a bit, but he does seem stressed. It breaks my heart."

Marty knelt down and caught sight of Dolto next to a laundry basket. "Hey guy," he said softly. "Are you looking for Emma?"

Dolto seemed to perk up at her name. He approached Marty cautiously, leaning in to sniff.

"I think he understood you," Lucy said.

Marty looked back at her, a wide smile on his face. "I think he did, too."

"There's no sense in you driving all the way back to the island, then coming here again. I think the right thing to do is for you to take him. Give him back to his Emma. I want him to be happy."

"Oh, that is – that would be – this is the most amazing news I've had all year," Marty said. He had the urge to hug the woman.

Juno clapped her hands together. "I'll get his carrier. Hopefully we can wrestle him in there."

Juno slipped away and Dolto took the opportunity to start rubbing his cheeks on Marty, first on his hands, then all over his legs. He started purring.

"I can't believe this," Marty said, turning to Lucy. "You're a genius."

She shrugged. "I've been telling you."

He laughed. He would never doubt Lucy again.

Juno returned a few minutes later. They were able to get Dolto into the carrier without much trouble. He was fairly easy-going.

"Promise to send me pictures when he's settled?" Juno asked.

"We promise," Lucy said, putting Juno's contact information into her phone. "Thank you again. For getting Dolto from Travis in the first place, and for this."

She nodded. "You're welcome."

"Can we give you anything?" Marty asked. He wasn't going to thrust thousands of dollars at her, though he'd be happy to. "Even to pay for his adoption supplies or something?"

"Heavens no!" She had tears in her eyes. "Head out now, or I'm going to break down right in front of you."

Marty didn't want to make the woman cry. "Thank you again. We'll be in touch!"

She walked them out, and Marty tucked the carrier carefully into his car before taking off.

Chapter Twenty-seven

Emma stayed at the top of the mountain for another hour. Once her unease about heights had worn off, she decided it was too beautiful for her to leave. She watched as the sun began its descent, setting the sky ablaze in red and orange.

It was getting quite cold then, so she returned to her car. Emma felt refreshed; she couldn't believe how much this little break had helped her.

Figuring out what to say to Marty would still be tough. He deserved to know that Becca had come to the island, and he deserved to know what she'd said. Emma even took a few notes when she got back to her car so she wouldn't forget anything.

Becca's guilt was palpable, though Emma knew it might be hard for Marty to understand at first. She couldn't pretend to relate to what he was going through, but she would encourage him to grant Becca some grace.

Once she was done making notes, she sent him a text saying she needed to talk to him.

"I need to talk to you, too," he said. "I have great news. I got Dolto, and I'm bringing him to you right now."

Emma stared at the screen. Was this a joke? "What do you mean?" she wrote back, hands cold.

Texting was silly. As soon as the text sent, she called him. He picked up right away.

"Hey Emma."

"Marty. Do you really have Dolto?"

"Yes. Travis gave him to a lady named Juno, and I was able to get him back just now."

"I helped!" Lucy's voice called out in the background.

Marty laughed. "Yeah, honestly, Lucy did most of the talking."

Emma had forgotten to breathe. She was getting dizzy and her limbs were tingling. "I can't believe this."

"He can't wait to see you," Lucy added. "He's healthy, too, so don't worry. Juno took good care of him."

"The only problem," Marty said, "is that we may not make the ferry tonight. But we'll be on the first one in the morning."

Emma looked around. Her hands were shaking. "I have work in the morning. Maybe I can get the day off?" She started her car, then tried to pull up a text to her boss all at once. She stopped herself. "No, actually, I should go to the store now and buy things for him. Unless this is a joke?"

"It's not a joke," Marty said. "We'll send you a picture. Lucy, can you take a picture?"

"Yeah yeah, one second. Emma, all you need to do is run to the store," Lucy said soothingly, "then call in sick to work."

Emma laughed. This was unbelievable. "I'm not going to fake being sick."

"Why not?" asked Lucy. "You get three free passes a year, I'm pretty sure."

"From Lucy, employee of the month," Marty added.

Emma bit her lip. "I'll see what I can do. I'm going to go to the store now, I think."

"Okay, talk to you later," Marty replied.

She hung up the phone and realized she'd completely forgotten to say thank you. She sent Marty a text apologizing to him and thanking him profusely. Hopefully Lucy was handling his messages, since he was driving. A moment later, a picture rolled in from Lucy.

It was Dolto! Tucked away and scowling in a carrier, but it was really him!

Shoot, Emma had forgotten to tell Marty about Becca. Her mind was going a mile a minute. She told herself to stop and calm down. If she didn't regain some composure, she'd send her car off the mountain and have a whole new set of problems.

Sitting in her car, she made a list of things she needed to do and a list of things she needed to buy. She also made up her mind that it'd be best to talk to Marty about Becca when she saw him in person. The news would go over better that way.

For now, she needed to get to the store before it closed. Did Dolto still like the same food? She would buy a couple different brands just to be safe. She still had some of his favorite toys, but she wanted to get some new ones, of course. And a new laser!

Emma rushed to the store and quickly bought everything she thought she'd need: food, a bed, toys, a brush, a scratching post, two litter boxes – everything. Emma didn't care about her budget. It didn't matter. Dolto was finally coming home.

It seemed too good to be true, and she felt guilty for doubting Marty. She kept running over what she wanted to say to him, so engrossed in her thoughts that she almost ran a stop sign.

Maybe Marty had been right to keep her in the dark? If she'd known Dolto had been given away, she may have fallen to pieces.

It wasn't right that Marty hid it from her, but in some ways, he'd made it easier in the end. It was enough to forgive him. More than enough. She'd make him promise to never do it again, though.

When she got home, she called her boss at the daycare and explained the situation. Her boss said she might be able to give her a half day. Emma thanked her profusely, and told her she'd be waiting to hear back.

Her phone rang about half an hour later. It was Marty. "Hey Emma."

"Hey! I just got back from the store. How's everything?"

"Good, everything's good, but I'm really sorry, we aren't going to make it to the ferry in time. We're going to find a cat-friendly hotel for the night and try again in the morning."

Emma smiled. She could now at least keep her thoughts somewhat straight. "Marty, I don't know how to thank you. I don't know how you did it."

"It's the least I could do," he said. "I don't want you to worry, though. We're all good here. Dolto even ate a bit on the drive."

"That's great! Okay, I won't keep you tied up. Good luck finding a hotel."

"Thanks. Sleep tight."

Emma spent the next hour running around, cleaning, and getting things set up. She had endless energy. At one point, she burst into a fit of giggles. That mountain air had really done something to her.

Her boss called back late that evening and confirmed she was able to get coverage for a half day. All that was left to do was contact her landlord and let him know she was getting a cat.

That might have to wait until morning. It wouldn't be a problem, though. Ever since losing Dolto, Emma had made sure to only rent apartments that allowed cats, just in case she ever had the chance to bring him home.

It was tough getting to sleep, but Emma managed to get some rest before going into work early. Marty texted her that they made the second ferry of the day, which was perfect. She didn't end up leaving right on time; there was a biting incident between two of the kids, so Emma had to stay a tad late, leaving after writing the incident report and talking to the parents.

It didn't take long, though, and nothing could bring her spirits down. When she got home for the day, Marty and Lucy were already there, waiting in Marty's car.

She parked and ran over. "Hey!"

Marty rolled down his window. "Nice running into you here."

Emma beamed. "You too."

Lucy leaned over, coming into view. "Stop chitchatting and open the door so she can get her cat."

Emma laughed as Marty did as he was told. The doors unlocked with a clunk and Emma pulled the door open. Nestled safely in a cream-colored carrier sat Dolto, his back turned, his plump haunches facing her.

"Nice rump you have there, Dolty," she said quietly.

He shifted, but didn't turn to look at her.

"We had a heck of a time getting him in there this morning," Lucy said. "He decided he was done with the carrier after yesterday's drive."

Emma carefully lifted the carrier. "No more driving, buddy. You're home now."

"We missed the first ferry because of it," Lucy continued. "Well, it got canceled, but we would've missed it anyway. I'm glad to report, though, that he only scratched Marty and not me."

Emma smiled. "Sorry about that."

"Let's get him inside," Marty said, getting out of the car.

Emma nodded, fumbling with her keys and dropping them on the ground. Lucy picked them up and offered to open the door.

Emma was grateful. Her hands were shaky and she was scared she might lose Dolto at the last second somehow.

Thankfully, nothing went wrong. Lucy opened the door, they walked inside, and Marty made sure the door was locked before Emma set the carrier down and opened the door.

Dolto jumped out immediately, running to the couch.

Emma let out a squeal. "Dolto! You're acting like you own the place."

"He pretty much does," Lucy said with a shrug.

Emma knelt down so she was eye to eye with him. "I've missed you so much." Her voice cracked and tears flooded her vision. "I'm so sorry, buddy. I'm so sorry."

Dolto leaned forward and butted his head into hers, then rubbed his cheeks on Emma's face and hands. She laughed, petting his neck, and he emitted a low purr.

Emma couldn't stop the tears, but Dolto didn't seem to mind.

"I missed you so much," she said, again and again.

"I think we'll excuse ourselves," Lucy announced. "Do you mind if I send a video of your reunion to the lady who had Dolto?"

Emma stood and wiped her cheeks. She needed to keep it together in front of her guests. "No, please do. Was it hard for her to give him up?"

"It was hard for me to convince her at first," Marty said. "Lucy was a big help. I'll tell you about it later."

Emma nodded. "Okay. I need to talk to you, too, Marty."

"We'll catch up soon," he said with a warm smile. "Enjoy your day with Dolto."

They turned to leave and Lucy's phone rang. She let out a frustrated grunt. "I was just about to send this video to Juno, and now Gigi is calling me. Should I answer?"

Marty shrugged. "Sure."

Lucy let out a sigh. "Hey, Gigi. What's up?" Lucy's forehead furrowed. "What?"

Emma and Marty turned to look at her.

"We'll be right there." Lucy ended the call and tucked the phone into her pocket. "Gigi said Becca just walked into the hotel."

Chapter Twenty-eight

There was never a more frustrating time to obey the speed limit than that day. Marty kept catching himself going forty-five miles per hour, even though the limit was thirty-five, and promptly dropped to twenty-five driving through Moran State Park.

Agony.

"So how did you and Becca leave things again?" Lucy asked.

"We didn't." Marty let out a sigh as a gaggle of cyclists pulled out in front of him, slowly meandering down the road. "She told me not to tell anyone she was alive. She also said something about me ruining her life, so I left."

Lucy winced. "That's harsh."

"I guess she's gotten over me ruining her life, but not her habit of being a perpetually terrible mother."

"Ah," Lucy said slowly. "You might want to cool it on that. I mean, she's come all the way here, so clearly she's changed her mind. Maybe she was surprised to see you and reacted poorly."

Marty scoffed. "Surprised to see me? She's been sending me letters for months. What did she think would happen?"

"I don't know," Lucy shrugged. "How was she supposed to know you're a people-tracking wizard? I could see myself doing something like that. Not being sure what I wanted, not thinking about what I was doing, then being surprised at the outcome."

"Somehow I don't think you would treat your only child or your twin sister the way that she has."

Lucy rolled the window down and stuck her arm out. "Maybe, but still. You should give her a chance. You said she was afraid of being rejected by Claire, right?"

"I guess."

"If you treat her poorly, then you'll prove her right. You'll show her that she never should have come back."

Marty had the nagging feeling that Lucy was right, but he wasn't ready to accept it yet. He said nothing.

Lucy continued. "Sometimes we have to forgive people for not reacting in the perfect way, or for failing to be the perfect person in the moment."

"And sometimes we don't have to do anything."

"True." Lucy turned to look out the window. "Let's just hear what she has to say."

The fact of the matter was that despite Marty talking a big game about being angry at Becca, he still drove directly to the hotel. If he hadn't wanted to see her, he wouldn't have driven there like a madman. Lucy was at least partially right.

As soon as they parked, Lucy unbuckled her seat belt and begged him to get out of the car. "Come on, or I'm going to meet her without you."

"Maybe you should."

"Stop being a pouty baby and get out of the car." Lucy walked over to his window, moving as though she was going to rip the car door open.

Marty wondered if he had enough time to lock his door, but in his hesitation, she managed to open it.

He got out without another word and they walked into the lobby together. Gigi was behind the front desk, chewing gum with her mouth open.

"Where'd she go?" Lucy asked

Gigi made a face as though she were thinking, then said, "I don't know. I told her you were coming, and the next time I looked up, she was gone."

Lucy crossed her arms. "Gigi, have you ever thought about getting a new job?"

"Why?" she asked with a frown.

"No reason."

"Let's just go," Marty said. "She probably left."

"We should at least look around for her," Lucy said. "Let's check the restaurant. She could've gotten hungry."

Lucy's theory proved to be incorrect. There was no one resembling Becca – or Claire, for that matter – in the restaurant. They went out onto the patio next, with the same result.

"She's gone, Lucy," Marty said, hands in his pockets. "That's what she does. She disappears."

Lucy bit her lip and fidgeted with her hands. "I refuse to believe that."

She shielded her eyes from the sun and slowly spun, scanning the grounds. Marty was ready to walk back inside when Lucy called out. "There! Is that her?"

He narrowed his eyes. Walking down the shore path was a lady with long, graying hair.

Marty shrugged. "It could be. Can't tell from behind."

"Let's go!" Lucy said.

He followed, though he couldn't keep up with her pace. Lucy was practically sprinting. Or was she skipping?

When she reached the woman, she reached a hand out and tapped her on the shoulder. Marty was still fifteen feet behind them when the woman spun around.

"Becca?" Lucy asked.

"You got me," she responded, putting her hands up.

Lucy didn't hesitate. She threw her arms around Becca and hugged her tightly. "I can't believe this. I can't believe you're real." She pulled away to look at her face. "You *are* real! This is unbelievable. You're alive!"

Becca patted her on the shoulder. "I'm alive, I'm alive. Hey, you're alive too!"

"Do you know who I am?"

Becca nodded. "Of course. I'd know you anywhere, Lucy."

Lucy squealed, hugging her again. "I can't believe this."

Marty caught up. He couldn't believe it either. Lucy was welcoming her like she was a celebrity or something.

What was so special about Becca? The woman had abandoned her son and let her twin sister believe she was dead for almost thirty years. It was an achievement, sure, but it wasn't a good one.

Lucy broke her grasp and Becca locked eyes with Marty. "You ran off on me."

He crossed his arms. "I didn't want to risk ruining your life."

"Come on," she said, taking a step toward him. "I didn't mean that. I didn't mean that at all."

He stared at her. "Okay."

"I was more afraid that..." She let out a sigh. "That I would ruin *your* life. It had turned out so well. I didn't want to go messing it up."

"Yes," said Lucy. "Despite his surly demeanor, Marty is quite a nice person."

He shot her a look.

"I know he is," Becca said. "That's why I couldn't resist sending those letters. I managed to stay out of your life for so long, but then...I don't know what came over me. I saw that article in the paper and I wanted to get to know you. I still do, if you'll give me a chance."

Marty opened his mouth to respond, but nothing came out. Give her a chance? After the way she'd treated him? After the way she'd treated Claire?

"Give him some time to think about it," Lucy said, patting him on the shoulder. "Marty tends to make rash decisions when he's emotional."

Becca laughed. "You get that from me, you know."

Marty nodded. Maybe Lucy was right, for once.

Not for once. She was right a lot recently. He needed to think with a clear head before deciding how to respond. "I do need some time," he finally said.

"I can understand that," Becca said.

"Have you seen Claire yet?" asked Lucy.

Becca shook her head. "No. You know, I think I'll catch her another time."

"No, you won't," Lucy said, hooking her arm through Becca's. "She's waited too long for this."

"Does she know I'm here?" asked Becca.

"I don't think so," Lucy said. "Marty, can you call her and see where she is?"

Sure, why not. Let's ruin Claire's day too.

He didn't argue, though. He placed the call and the phone rang and rang, eventually going to voicemail. "She's not answering."

Lucy frowned. "I'm sure we can find her. The island isn't that big." Lucy kept walking toward the hotel, pulling Becca with her. "I'm so excited, I don't even know what to ask you."

Becca put a hand up. "I'm an open book, Lucy."

"Who's your favorite niece?" Lucy said before sputtering out a laugh. "I'm just kidding. I know it's me."

Becca laughed with her, and at that moment, when Marty was shooting a glare at them both, his phone went off. A message from Claire. "Sorry I missed your call. Everything okay?"

He wrote back. “I’m at the hotel. I have some news.”

“How exciting!” she wrote back. “Can’t wait to hear it. I’m in the office.”

He looked up at Lucy and Becca. They were walking slowly, arm in arm, chatting. Lucy might be able to accept this without question, but it would surely be harder for Claire.

He thought Claire deserved a warning before her dead sister came waltzing through her door.

“Hey guys,” he called out, “Claire is in her office. I’m going to run ahead and prepare her so she doesn’t have a heart attack.”

“Good thinking,” Lucy yelled back. “You’ve got ten minutes starting...now!”

He shook his head, but he knew Lucy wasn’t joking and picked up his pace. Claire should know the truth. It was long overdue.

Chapter Twenty-nine

There were only a few details left to straighten out for the Fruit Festival. Claire couldn't believe it was finally happening in just ten short days. It seemed like they'd been planning it for years.

A week couldn't pass without one problem or another rearing its ugly head. Most recently there had been a hiccup with the ribbons for the pie and jam contest winners. Claire was prepared to fashion them out of makeshift ribbons herself, but at the last minute, the company confirmed they'd send them in time.

She sat back in her chair and smiled. Lillian and Rose were planning to make the trip to enjoy the festivities. Claire couldn't wait. It was going to be so much fun! Who knew event planning would be one of her strengths?

There was a knock at the door and Claire suddenly remembered Marty's text. "Come in!" she called out.

He stepped inside, his face taut and serious. "Hey, Claire."

Oh dear, he didn't look happy. "Is something wrong?"

He shook his head. "No, don't worry. Nothing bad. Do you mind if I take a seat?"

"Please."

He settled in the chair across from her, shoulders hunched and his head angled down. After a moment, he looked up. "You remember those letters I got?"

"Yes." How could she forget? She thought about them all the time.

"I found out who's been sending them."

A chill ran down her spine. "Go on."

He sat back, rubbing his hands together. "I don't know how to tell you this."

"Just spit it out, Marty," she said with a nervous laugh.

"Claire." He stood up and paced across the room twice before speaking again. "It was Becca."

An anvil hit her stomach. "Becca?"

He nodded, taking a seat again. "Yes. I met her. I talked to her. It was her."

"That's impossible," Claire said, not believing the words even as they left her mouth.

Marty kept talking, but Claire couldn't hear him. It was as though her ears had disconnected from her brain. Marty's voice became background noise, like the droning of a ship's engine. She was carried further and further away, seemingly lost at sea.

"Claire? Are you okay?"

She snapped her head back toward him. She hadn't realized her eyes had zoned out, too, and she was staring at the wall. "Yeah, I'm fine. Sorry."

"It's okay. I can't imagine how shocking this is. I can't imagine how angry you are."

She tilted her head to the side. “Angry?”

There was another knock at the door. Claire looked over, then back at Marty. “Do you know who that is?”

He nodded, slowly standing up. “It’s Becca. She’s here. She just showed up. I’m sorry. If it’s too much I can send her away.”

“No, it’s okay. I want to see her.” Claire stood from her chair and straightened her blouse.

Marty offered a weak smile. “I’m sorry all of this is happening so fast.”

Claire nodded and walked over to the door, taking a deep breath before pulling it open.

It was Lucy. “Do you mind if I come in?”

“No, not at all.”

Lucy stepped inside. “I have someone else with me. I’m not sure if Marty told you?”

Claire nodded. “He did.”

“Maybe we should go?” Marty said to Lucy. “We can wait out in the lobby.”

“Good idea.” Lucy gave Claire a hug. “We’ll be waiting for you, okay?”

Claire nodded. Her throat was too dry to speak. She watched as they walked out the door, and a third figure came into view behind the door’s frosted glass.

She pulled the door open fully, setting eyes on none other than her twin sister.

Claire’s mouth popped open. She wanted to say something, but she found herself unable to form any words.

Becca smiled a small, sheepish smile, and looked down. "Hey, Claire Bear."

Claire burst into tears, and a moment later, Becca did, too. As sobs racked her body, Claire stepped forward and hugged her sister.

All these years wishing she could see Becca one last time, to tell her how much she loved her, to tell her how sorry she was – the moment had come, and it had turned her into an absolute puddle.

It took a full fifteen minutes for them to calm down and actually speak. Claire had a box of tissues, which they tore through quickly, and they shared her bottle of water.

Becca was the first to form a full sentence. "I didn't know if you'd want to see me."

Claire was astonished by this. "Of course I do. Becca, I've been missing you for years. I've missed you so much."

Becca looked down at the ground. "I've missed you too. I'm sorry. I'm so sorry. For everything."

Claire offered her the last sip of water, which she accepted. "This doesn't seem real. Am I dreaming?"

"Only if I am too," Becca said with a laugh. "I know it's no excuse, but I've been afraid all this time. I was so afraid..."

Fear pushes people into the wrong decisions. Claire knew that. She reached across the table and grabbed her sister's hand. "I'm sorry you felt that way. I know I was always hard on you, and you didn't deserve it. You don't know how I've wished that I had been kinder, more understanding – "

"No, I deserved it. All of it." Becca squeezed her hand. "I don't expect you to forgive me."

"There's nothing to forgive. You're my sister."

Becca pinched her lips together, tears springing to her eyes. "I didn't know about the plane crash for months."

"Really?" Claire sat back.

Becca hurriedly wiped the tears on the back of her hand. "When they came to get me, I almost got on the plane with them. There's no excuse, but I ran off at the last minute. I couldn't face Mom or Dad or Holly. I couldn't tell them about Marty, about failing rehab, so I ran off. Hitchhiked and shacked up with some people I met at the rehab center."

Claire let out a breath. "I see."

"I think it was six months later, when I came out of that haze, that I found out what had happened." Becca rubbed her face with her hands. "I felt so awful, Claire. I still feel awful. I know it was my fault that they died."

"It was an accident," Claire said. Some small part of her used to blame Becca for the accident, but no longer. Not now, seeing her in the flesh, all regret and heartache and pain.

"It was my fault. I knew it then, and I know it now." Becca sighed heavily. "After that, I went back to my selfish ways. I felt sorry for myself. I was in a spiral for years. *Years*."

Claire wrung her hands together. "I wish you could've told me."

"I almost did, a thousand times. I told myself that I would straighten myself out, get clean. That I would find you and the girls. But every time I even thought about coming to see you, I couldn't do it. I fell back off the wagon and had to start over again."

Poor Becca. Claire didn't know what to say.

"It took me thirteen years, Claire. Thirteen years before I got on the right path. Once I was straightened out, with a job and everything... I was still too afraid. I thought it would be worse to bring an old ghost into your life. I thought you were doing better without me."

"Oh, Becca," Claire whispered. "I've never been whole without you. I wish I could've helped."

"You couldn't." She shook her head. "That was the thing. That was always the thing." Becca flashed a pained smile. "It wasn't until I saw Marty getting chased by the FBI that I thought *hey, why don't I reach out?* He's the one person whose life I didn't ruin. Or so I thought. I think he hates me. Can't blame him."

"He doesn't hate you, and no one else does either," Claire said firmly. "He's young. He doesn't know that life is short and it's better to forgive the people we love."

"I hope I can live up to that. I'm trying, at least."

The tears came back to Claire's eyes. "Becca, I wish I'd made this clear when we were young. I love you just as you are. Always, okay?"

Becca nodded, then wiped her nose on the back of her hand. "Got any more of those tissues?"

Claire smiled. "If I'd known you were coming, I would've bought a whole case."

Chapter Thirty

More than once, Marty considered leaving the hotel lobby and going home. He wasn't particularly interested in talking to Becca, and he had other things on his mind. What was supposed to have been a wonderful day was tainted by Becca's visit.

Emma and Dolto were reunited, though. Nothing could spoil that.

He stood and Lucy sat up to address him. "Where do you think you're going?"

Marty shrugged. "Home."

"No you're not," she said simply. "Sit down."

He should've known it wouldn't be easy. "Thanks again for your help."

She stared up at him. "For what?"

"With Dolto. You were right. I needed help. I thought I could just show up and offer to pay for him, but I was way off base."

Lucy tapped her forehead. "See, you needed me! You discounted the emotional aspect."

"I guess I did."

She slouched in her seat, taking up nearly the entire length of the antique chaise. "I didn't think that someone would adopt a middle-aged cat off Facebook for the money. There had to be something else."

"You were right. Though Dolto's not middle-aged. He's only a few years old."

Lucy made a face. "Don't cats age like dogs? Seven times as fast?"

"I don't think so," he said. "I don't think dogs age that way, either. Cats can live eighteen years."

"Eighteen years!" Lucy, who had started slipping down the couch, now sat up. "That's a long time. Maybe I should get a cat."

"Do you like cats?" asked Marty.

Lucy shrugged. "I liked Dolto, especially when he had his claws in your arm. That was funny."

"I'm glad you enjoyed it." He laughed. The scratches weren't bad. He'd certainly seen worse.

Poor Dolto had been afraid, but now hopefully he'd never feel fear again. Emma would take care of him.

"You know," Lucy said, "I've never been an animal person, so I don't think I really *get* it, but I get what you did."

"What do you mean?"

"That getting Dolto back was an act of love."

"All right." Marty let out a sigh. "I'm going to go."

"Please don't! I'll stop!" She flashed an eager smile. "Ten more minutes, and then you can go."

"Fine." He plopped back into his seat and pulled his phone out to see he had a slew of messages from Emma. There were pictures of Dolto, looking much happier, and a stack of thank yous.

Emma's last message read, "I know this doesn't at all cover it, but maybe I could take you to dinner as a thanks?"

Marty didn't think she owed him anything. He didn't get Dolto because he was trying to win her over. Not really. It wasn't like he wanted anything from her.

He just admired her so much and he hated to see her in pain. Emma deserved to be happy. She deserved to be free of Travis. The fact that he was in love with her was more of an inconvenience than anything.

It was time to come clean. Not about being in love with her – understandably, she wanted nothing to do with that. He wouldn't foist his feelings onto her. Emma deserved peace.

Yet it was time to come clean about his other sins. He needed to tell Emma that he was likely the one that got Travis fired. She'd be upset, but he didn't want to hide anything from her anymore.

He agreed to have dinner with her that night, suggesting they get takeout and eat at her place so she wouldn't have to leave Dolto. Emma liked that plan.

After more than an hour, Claire and Becca emerged from the office. They both had red eyes and red noses. It made them look even more alike, though the rest of them couldn't be more different.

Becca was dressed in a long, orange skirt that swished every time she walked. Her mane-like hair was messy and wild, just like her.

Claire was like a Becca from an alternate universe. She looked like she'd walked out of a magazine, maybe even a fancy hotel magazine. She matched the hotel perfectly. The idea of Claire trading her little sweaters and high heels for Becca's hippie clothing made Marty smile. It was so absurd.

"Sorry about the wait," Claire said. "We had a lot to catch up on."

"I bet you did!" said Lucy. "Now what are we going to do?"

Claire looked at Becca, then laughed. "I have no idea!"

"Anything we want, I guess," Becca added.

Marty stared at them. It wasn't until now that he realized how similar their voices were. The only difference was that Becca's sounded raspy, like she had a cold.

"Any ideas, Marty?" Lucy asked.

He stared at her, arms crossed. Was she really going to welcome Becca like this, with no questions asked? "I don't know."

"It's okay to take some time," said Becca.

"Thanks for the permission, I guess?" Marty replied.

Lucy cleared her throat. "Aunt Becca, how about I take you to the restaurant in the hotel? Are you hungry?"

"I can always eat," she said, flashing a smile.

Lucy hooked arms with her and led her away. "You two are welcome to join," she called over her shoulder.

Claire laughed and waved a hand. "I'll catch up in a few."

She turned toward Marty and the look on her face made his stomach sink. "Why does it feel like I'm about to get a talking-to?"

"Because you are," Claire said, hands on her hips. "What's going on, Marty? Why are you so angry?"

Marty's jaw dropped. "Are you serious? Aren't you angry with Becca? She killed your whole family, and then left you to raise three kids on your own."

"No, Marty." Claire's voice was soft, but firm. "It's not as simple as all that."

He couldn't believe what he was hearing! "I thought you'd be angry and never want to see her. I mean, am I the crazy one here?"

"Don't hold a grudge on my behalf," Claire said carefully. "I'm not angry at her. I thought she was dead, Marty. Do you know how many regrets I've had over the years?"

"I guess I don't," he said, lowering his voice.

She reached out a hand and squeezed his shoulder. "I'd already lost her for all that time. I refuse to lose one more day by being upset with her."

He frowned. That was one way to look at it.

She continued. "I don't know what our relationship is going to be like, but I'm glad she came back. She was afraid to face me after all this time. It makes me feel awful. If only I had known."

Marty shook his head. "It's not your fault, Claire. It's hers."

"Like I said, don't hold a grudge on my behalf. This is one of the best days of my life." Claire smiled, her eyes filling with tears.

He raised an eyebrow. "Really?"

She laughed. "Really. I can understand if you don't want a relationship with her, not right now. That's fine. Take some time to think about it, okay? Just remember, Marty, life isn't easy. We don't always make the right decisions. Even you might make a mistake one day."

Marty frowned. He was great at making mistakes. "I'm sorry. You're right."

"I'm going to have lunch with them, and there's no pressure for you to join, but you're welcome."

Marty hesitated. If he went, it might be uncomfortable. If he didn't go...

Claire was right. He had nothing to lose but time with this mysterious woman. "All right. I'm coming."

Her face brightened into a smile. "Wonderful!"

Marty's fears were unfounded. Lunch wasn't awkward in the least. That was mostly due to Lucy's nonstop commentary, but also because of Becca. There was an uncanny similarity between Becca and Lucy, and once Marty noticed it, he couldn't unsee it.

It was disturbing, especially considering that Lucy had no qualms about welcoming Becca into the family. Perhaps what Lucy had said earlier was true. Becca's actions made sense to her.

The thought made Marty feel odd. He wanted to dismiss it. It was obvious that Lucy didn't take after Claire, but Marty had assumed she got her big personality from her mom or dad or something.

Now it was staring him in the face: Lucy was like her Aunt Becca. And if Marty liked Lucy, surely he could learn to like Becca?

He was willing to consider it, but it was too much for one day. At the end of their meal, Becca and Claire decided to go into town together. Lucy announced she was going to let them have time alone together, and Marty decided it was a chance for him to take a break from socializing. He needed time to think and recharge.

When he got home, he was exhausted, but there were some tasks he needed to do for work. He opened his computer and managed to focus for the next few hours.

Once he caught up, he reached out to Emma. He offered to pick up their dinner so she wouldn't need to leave the house.

"That's so sweet of you," she said. "That'd be great."

He felt nervous heading over to her place. He hoped she wouldn't be too angry about what he'd done to Travis's email.

It was a strange thing to do. Perhaps Becca was right about him taking after her in one way – making rash decisions. It was an unfortunate pattern in his life.

When he got to Emma's apartment, she opened the door quickly.

"Thanks so much, Marty."

"No problem." He set the food on her small kitchen table. "How's Dolto?"

Emma smiled broadly. "He's great. I think he got spooked when the door opened, but he'll come out in a few minutes."

Emma was right. As soon as they started setting the table, Dolto made himself known. He walked along the back of the couch until he was standing directly behind Marty, then meowed.

Marty spun around. "Hey man!" He reached out a hand and gave Dolto a few scratches under the chin, which the cat accepted happily. Dolto jumped off the couch and bounded toward Emma, weaving through her legs as she walked between the kitchen and the table.

"Dolto," she laughed. "I'll pick you up after I eat. Okay, bud?"

He continued following her, unsatisfied with this deal.

Marty got two glasses of water and took a seat at the table. "Lucy told me that Juno, the lady who had Dolto, really loved the video of you guys reuniting. She said it made her cry."

"I'm sure," Emma said with a laugh. "I was crying like a baby!"

He smiled. "Understandable."

"Honestly, I can't thank you enough. I'm so sorry I got angry at you. I know this doesn't make up for it, but I hope it's a start."

He waved a hand. "Please. I deserved it. I should've told you about Dolto as soon as I had any information. You deserved to know. That was a huge mistake, and I'm really sorry."

She sat down across from him. "That wasn't my favorite part of it, no." Emma let out a little laugh. "I'll just ask that you not hide things from me in the future."

"I won't."

"Thanks." She popped the lid to her meal. "Still, you got him back. I wasn't able to do it for years, but you did in a few weeks."

"Lucy was the one who talked Juno into it. She was suspicious of me, but not of Lucy."

Emma smiled. "I like Lucy."

"Me too." He set his fork down. "Speaking of being honest, there's something else I have to tell you."

Emma took a bite of her fried rice and made a face. "That's ominous."

"This is pretty bad. Not as bad as hiding Dolto from you, but not great."

"Okay." Emma folded her hands in front of her. "What is it?"

He took a sip of water. "I think I'm the one who got Travis fired."

Emma choked on a laugh. "Are you serious?"

"Yes. After we had that whole email thing. Still sorry about that, by the way."

She shook her head. "Still not a big deal."

He looked down. "I might have, sort of, hacked into his email."

Emma put a hand over her mouth. "Marty, you didn't!"

"I did." He looked up at her. At least she didn't seem livid. Not yet. "I wanted to see if there were any more emails about Dolto. It was totally innocent. Sort of."

Emma started eating again. "Right."

Marty kept talking. He was on a roll now. "There wasn't anything in there about him, not really. But there was a rude email that Travis wrote about his boss, and I might've forwarded it to the entire staff."

Emma leaned forward. "*Marty!* I think you can go to jail for stuff like that."

"Yeah, probably," he said, taking his first bite of food. "Sometimes I get these ideas and I don't question them enough, you know? I'm realizing that I tend to make emotional decisions."

"I can see that," Emma said, her brown eyes locked onto his. "Is that all?"

"Yes," he said slowly. "I thought you'd be upset."

She looked up toward the ceiling, as though she were carefully thinking about what he'd said. "Nope!"

"That's a relief," Marty said, taking a large swig of water. He could feel the adrenaline leaving his body.

"Maybe I would've been upset before," Emma said. "But after what he did to Dolto...I don't know."

Marty sat up straighter. Was she finally seeing Travis for what he was?

She bit her lip. "For the longest time, I made excuses for Travis. You were right, though. He can be mean, and there's no excuse for it. If he didn't want Dolto anymore, he could have given him to me. He gave him away to a stranger on purpose. He wanted to hurt me."

Marty nodded. "I know. It made me irrationally angry."

"I don't want to see what you do when you're rationally angry," Emma said with a smile.

He shook his head. "It's never happened, so don't worry."

They both laughed.

Emma's smile faded and she let out a sigh. "I have something to tell you, too. I was waiting until we could talk in person."

"Oh?"

She shifted in her seat. "I don't want you to get upset with me, because this was a freak sort of thing."

"Okay..."

"Yesterday Claire gave me a half day off, and I decided to go to Mount Constitution."

"That's great! Was it a clear day?"

She nodded. "It was gorgeous. I went to the top of the observation tower and I met someone there."

Marty's heart sank. This was it. She was going to tell him that she met a great guy and they were in love and they were running off to get married. "Yeah?"

Emma winced. "It was your mom."

"My mom?" Marty sat back. "I didn't know she was here. She was supposed to come visit next month."

Emma stared at him for a beat, then said, "Oh, I'm sorry. I met your other mom. Becca?"

"Ah." That made more sense.

"I didn't realize that you had met her, too," Emma said, the speed of her speech increasing with every sentence. "She was telling me she had come all the way here, but she wasn't going to look for you. I might've said some things."

Marty smiled. "Like what?"

"I took some notes, but now I can't find them. Basically, she had this whole spiel about how she wasn't going to come here and ruin your lives, and...I don't know. I was so annoyed. I told her if she was too scared to meet you, then she didn't deserve to know you."

Marty stared at her. He no longer felt sick. Maybe just lovesick.

"I'm sorry. I probably shouldn't have told her anything," Emma said. "I just thought it was so crummy that she came all the way here and she was just going to give up."

"She took your advice. She came to the hotel."

Emma's eyes widened. "That was really her, then?"

Marty nodded and told her the story of their meeting. He finished with, "I'm going to try to take Claire's advice and get to know her. It's just strange, you know?"

"I am so happy for you," Emma said, clapping her hands together. There were tears in her eyes. "I know this isn't how you imagined it, but this is great news. For all of you. It will give your family a chance to heal."

That was a nice way to put it. Emma always put things in nice ways. "Thanks."

They finished eating, consciences clear, and after, Emma bent down and scooped Dolto up from the floor. "He's such a cuddle monster."

"I'm glad you can be together again." He stood from his seat, clearing the containers from the table. "I'd better get going. You two have a lot to catch up on."

Her eyes lingered on him for a moment before responding. "Have a good night, Marty."

Chapter Thirty-one

As soon as the door closed behind him, Emma's heart sunk. Why had she been such a chicken? Why hadn't she asked him why he was so determined to get Dolto back for her?

Was it really just because he had a temper? He said as much. He said it was because he didn't like seeing what Travis had done.

It had nothing to do with him liking her. She and Marty were friends, after all. Perhaps Marty treated all of his friends that way.

But maybe he didn't.

She set Dolto down and quickly put her shoes on. "Stay here, buddy. I'll be right back."

She ran out the front door, almost tripping when she spotted Marty's car. She waved her arms and yelled, "Wait!"

Thankfully, he caught sight of her before he pulled away and rolled his window down. "Is everything okay?"

She bit her lip. "No."

"Is it Dolto?" he asked, eyes wide.

"No. It's..." She shook her head. What was she going to say to him? What had gotten into her?

Marty got out of the car. "What's going on?"

She felt so silly, but if she didn't say anything, she would feel even worse. "Why did you try so hard to get Dolto back?"

"I don't know." Marty scratched his head.

She looked down. "I didn't know if it was because we're friends or because we're something more."

Emma looked back up at Marty. His mouth was hanging open.

"I'm sorry," she said. "I didn't mean to – "

"No." He stepped closer. "I know you said you weren't looking to date anyone. I respect that."

Emma wanted to laugh. "I didn't mean *you*."

"What?" He cocked his head to the side.

She stared at him.

After a moment, a smile spread across his face and he threw his head back and laughed. "Emma, I've been in love with you since the moment I saw you at Blaise's house."

Now *that* she wasn't expecting. "What?"

"It's been impossible. I made peace with being your friend, because I love being around you. I didn't want to bother you with how I felt."

"Bother me?" She shook her head. "All this time I thought you didn't like me."

He grabbed both of her hands. "No. I'm just... " He shook his head, eyes shining. "I'm bad at expressing myself. At communicating! Lucy makes fun of me for it."

Emma felt like she was floating. "I had no idea, Marty."

"Man." He sighed. "All this time I was worried I was making you uncomfortable."

She squeezed his hands. "You never make me uncomfortable. I didn't think I was capable of dating again, but with you, everything feels different."

He took a step closer to her. "Everything is different with you, too. Usually if I get a crush on someone, it fades away the more I get to know them. With you, it just got worse and worse. I fell more in love with you every day."

Emma thought her cheeks would crack from smiling. "Tell me again."

"I'm in love with you," he said, voice low.

She dropped her voice to a whisper. "I'm in love with you, too."

He took his hands and gently placed them on the sides of her face. Emma closed her eyes. A moment later, all of her fears were erased as he kissed her.

What a day.

Epilogue

Though Claire wouldn't agree to let Lucy be a pie-baking contest judge at the Fruit Festival, she still got to try many of the pies. Truth be told, she couldn't judge the difference between first place, an apple cobbler pie, and second place, a blackberry meringue. They were both excellent. Why did they need to pick favorites?

Both of the bakers lived and worked on the island, too. Lucy had initially planned to steal slices and run away, but she ended up caught in conversation.

"Have you ever seen our farm?" asked Fiona, the first-place winner.

Lucy shook her head, her mouth full of pie. "No, but I'd love to visit."

"You have to come! We have acres of orchards. We make apple butter and baked goods. During the winter, we make cider and apple whiskey."

Lucy raised an eyebrow. "Is that an award winner too?"

"Not to brag, but yes, it is."

Impressive. "Are you hiring?"

Fiona's eyes brightened. "We are, actually. Are you interested?"

This would be the most nonchalant way Lucy had ever gotten a job. “Maybe?”

“Stop on by, then,” Fiona said with a warm smile.

Marty waved her over from across the field. “Excuse me,” Lucy said.

She moved toward Marty slowly, careful not to drop the rest of her pie. The ice cream on her plate was melting quickly, sliding around like a mad glob. She needed to eat it as fast as she could.

“Do you mind being in charge of the history tent for a bit?” Marty asked when she reached him. “Emma said she’s on her way and I wanted to show her around.”

Lucy reached forward and pinched his cheek. “I don’t mind taking over so you can see your *girlfriend*.”

Marty shooed her hand away. “All right, all right.” He smiled. “Thanks, Lucy.”

That was one couple who had taken way too long getting together. They were both so shy. Maybe that was why?

Lucy could never get it to work with shy guys. She scared them away. Come to think of it, she scared the non-shy guys, too. She was just scary.

“Save some pie for everybody else,” said a voice.

Lucy turned around to see Becca approaching. “Don’t you start with me. There’s plenty to go around.”

“You’re right. I don’t even really like pie.”

“You’re sick,” Lucy said, stuffing the last bite into her mouth.

"Have you seen Claire anywhere?"

Lucy shook her head. "No. She's been running around putting out fires."

"Fires?"

Lucy waved a hand. "Not literal fires. Figurative fires. She loves it. She acts like she doesn't, but she lives for it."

Becca let out a sigh. "This whole event fills me with awe. It's magnificent. Look at all these happy faces. Everything Claire does is impressive. Always was."

Lucy shrugged. "That's her. Don't take it personally."

Becca laughed. "I'll try to see if I can help out."

The rest of the day went well. Lillian and Rose were no help, running around like tourists, but Lucy did her duty at the historical tent. She was surprised to see that young and old alike were enjoying the exhibits.

There were pictures and displays on loan to them by the Orcas Historical Society, as well as some pictures and artifacts loaned by native tribes. That was all Chip's doing. He'd wanted to highlight his heritage.

People were fascinated by it. Lucy was, too. She happily spent the next few hours playing guide to the island's history.

It wasn't until that evening that Lucy was able to find Claire. She was tucked away in the office, a frown fixed on her face.

"Another crisis?" Lucy asked as she flopped on a chair. She'd eaten so much pie that it felt like her stomach would explode.

"I'm not sure," Claire said.

Chip let out a huff and paced across the room. "I'm sure it's fine."

The site of him made Lucy startle. "I didn't know you were in here, Chip!"

He put his hands on his hips. "It's my office, too."

Lucy made a face. "Yeah, but, you know."

"I don't. What?"

"It's not *really* your office. I also come here to paint my nails sometimes, or to watch movies."

Chip's jaw dropped in mock shock, but before he could answer, Claire waved a hand at them. "That's enough out of you two. Chip, it was sort of like you were hiding in the corner."

"You were," Lucy said, nodding

He took a seat, quietly countering, "Was not." Claire shot him a look and he laughed. "Sorry. You're right. Now isn't a time to joke."

"It's not funny, Chip!" Claire said. "That guy gave me a bad feeling."

"What guy?" Lucy's eyes darted between them. Chip still looked jovial, probably still riding the high from the successful Fruit Festival. Claire did not share his glee. "Did someone make off with all the jam?"

"No, it's much worse than that," Claire said. "A man approached us at one of the berry stands."

"Yes, the berry stand." Lucy nodded solemnly. "A dangerous place."

Claire continued. "He said he was impressed with the festival, and he wanted to buy the hotel."

Lucy raised an eyebrow. "How much?"

"Three million dollars," Chip said.

Lucy scoffed. "Yeah right. The hotel's worth a lot more than that. Did you punch him in the nose?"

"No, Lucy, we did not resort to violence." Claire was not in the joking mood. "I thanked him for his offer but told him we're not interested in selling. And he leaned in and whispered in my ear – "

Lucy interrupted again. "Ew! Whispered in your ear?"

Claire nodded. "Yes. He said that I should reconsider, because if I don't accept his offer, he would take the hotel from me. The hard way."

"The hard way?" Lucy looked at Chip, who was no longer smiling. "What's that supposed to mean?"

"I don't know," Claire said. "But I didn't like the sound of it. I didn't like how he smiled at me before he walked away."

"He was bluffing," Chip said unconvincingly. "There's no way for him to do that. He's just a whacko."

Lucy let out a sigh. "Maybe he was just trying to ruin the fun, maybe he's going to pull something. There's nothing we can do now, though, is there?"

"I'm thinking I'll contact an attorney to be sure," Claire said.

Lucy jumped up from her seat. "Good idea. So now that man is officially no longer today's problem. He's tomorrow's problem."

Claire laughed. "That's a very Lucy way of thinking about things."

"What can I say? I live for the moment. They're serving sparkling sugarplum champagne in the lobby. And there's going to be a reading from *Lummi Elders Speak*. Are you guys really going to miss it to worry about some creepy whisperer?"

Claire closed the folder in front of her and smiled. "Of course not."

"Good thinking, Lucy." Chip stood and gallantly offered his arm to Claire. "Let's have some sparkling sugarplum fairy champagne."

"No one said anything about fairies," Lucy said, shaking her head and pulling open the door. "But if that makes you feel better, sure."

The Next Chapter

Introduction to *Sunset Tides*

There's such a fine line between love and disdain...

Lucy Woodley's move to Orcas Island was exciting...at first. She made friends, enjoyed the sights, and tried to embrace her new job at a local farm. But Lucy isn't one for routine, and just as island life starts to get a bit boring, a new challenge arrives: Rob Coolidge.

Rob has no interest in small town living. His goal is simple: make money for his company, and get a promotion - even if it means killing a family farm to do it. Rob is used to making tough decisions, and this business opportunity on Orcas is no different. He's not going to let sentimentality or flighty Lucy get in his way.

Lucy vows to stop him and his arrogant money-hungry ways. The only problem? His good looks and charm start to wear her down, and the lines of disdain start to blur into respect. Will Rob change his ways in time to win Lucy over, or will he betray her at the last moment?

Get your copy of the third installment of the Orcas Island series today!

Would you like to join my reader group?

Sign up for my reader newsletter and get a free copy of my novella Christmas at Saltwater Cove. You can sign up by visiting: https://bit.ly/XmasSWC

About the Author

Amelia Addler writes always sweet, always swoon-worthy romance stories and believes that everyone deserves their own happily ever after.

Her soulmate is a man who once spent five weeks driving her to work at 4AM after her car broke down (and he didn't complain, not even once). She is lucky enough to be married to that man and they live in Pittsburgh with their little yellow mutt. Visit her website at AmeliaAddler.com or drop her an email at amelia@AmeliaAddler.com.

Also by Amelia...

The Orcas Island Series

Sunset Cove

Sunset Secrets

Sunset Tides

The Westcott Bay Series

Saltwater Cove

Saltwater Studios

Saltwater Secrets

Saltwater Crossing

Saltwater Falls

Saltwater Memories

Saltwater Promises

Christmas at Saltwater Cove

Standalone Novels

The Summer Request

Made in the USA
Columbia, SC
19 June 2024

b5915a58-b9fd-4fdb-9d1e-6816999133efR01